# SQUARING THE CIRCLE

*by the same author*

ROSENCRANTZ AND GUILDENSTERN ARE DEAD

THE REAL INSPECTOR HOUND

ENTER A FREE MAN

AFTER MAGRITTE

JUMPERS

TRAVESTIES

DIRTY LINEN and NEW-FOUND-LAND

NIGHT AND DAY

DOGG'S HAMLET, CAHOOT'S MACBETH

UNDISCOVERED COUNTRY
(*a version of Arthur Schnitzler's*
Das weite Land)

ON THE RAZZLE
(*adapted from Johann Nestroy's*
Einen Jux will er sich machen)

THE REAL THING

THE DOG IT WAS THAT DIED
*and other plays*

FOUR PLAYS FOR RADIO
Artist Descending a Staircase
Where Are They Now?
If You're Glad I'll be Frank
Albert's Bridge

*and a novel*

LORD MALQUIST AND MR MOON

# SQUARING THE CIRCLE

BY

# TOM STOPPARD

WITH

### EVERY GOOD BOY
### DESERVES FAVOUR

AND

### PROFESSIONAL FOUL

*faber and faber*

LONDON · BOSTON

*Every Good Boy Deserves Favour* and *Professional Foul*
first published in 1978
*Squaring the Circle* first published in 1984
This collection first published in 1984
by Faber and Faber Limited
3 Queen Square London WC1N 3AU

Filmset by Wilmaset
Birkenhead Merseyside
Printed in Great Britain by
Whitstable Litho Limited
Whitstable Kent
All rights reserved

*British Library Cataloguing in Publication Data*

Stoppard, Tom
Squaring the circle; Professional foul;
Every good boy deserves favour
I. Title
II. Stoppard, Tom. Professional foul
III. Stoppard, Tom. Every good boy deserves favour
822'.914    PR6069.T6
ISBN 0-571-13408-4
ISBN 0-571-13095-X Pbk

# CONTENTS

# INTRODUCTION

At the beginning of 1982, about a month after the imposition of martial law in Poland, a film producer named Fred Brogger suggested that I should write a television film about Solidarity. Thus began a saga, only moderately exceptional by these standards, which may be worth recounting as an example of the perils which sometimes attend the offspring of an Anglo-American marriage.

Fred started by taking on a professional researcher. Soon I was in possession of tens of thousands of facts about Poland but it was far from clear what had to be done with them. They took in everything from a summary of 600 years of Polish history to the make of General Jaruzelski's car (a BMW). Naturally, the more detailed the information the more questions were left begging. What *colour* was the BMW? It was green. Excellent. But what colour was the upholstery? The demand for an ever more powerful telescope was accompanied by the demand for an ever more sensitive bugging device. Many of Lech Walesa's statements were on record, some of them actually on tape, a state of affairs which tempted one towards documentary reconstruction without the possibility of fulfilment.

We had a meeting in the middle of February. The minutes (this was an efficient operation) state: 'The principal problem, Tom feels, is that we don't *know* what happened and what was said. . . . Whatever he portrays will be taken as fact rather than as "fiction" by his audience unless there is some form of disclaimer or a dramatic device which will make it clear. . . .'

This was becoming my main worry. Documentary fiction, by definition, is always in danger of seeming to claim to know more than a film maker *can* know. Accurate detail mingles with arty detail, without distinguishing marks, and history mingles with good and bad guesses. One example which we kept coming back to

9

was the character of General Jaruzelski. At that time, and perhaps still, opinion was divided. Some saw him as a hard liner, Moscow's Man; others saw him as a 'patriot' forced into a tough Polish solution to stave off a tougher Russian one. We tended to think of him as a 'moderate'. I recall that this judgement was based on one concrete fact which kept cropping up in the research material: Jaruzelski, as Minister of Defence, had once refused to order Polish soldiers to fire on Polish workers. Two years later, soon after the film containing this fact was in the can, I learned that new information tended to consign the 'fact' to myth. It was the fear of just such imponderables and just such confusion between large speculations and small truths (the wrong Jaruzelski in the right car) that led me to the idea of having a narrator with *acknowledged fallibility*.

The meeting ended with a hopeful diary date for the transmission of the film – 13 December, the first anniversary of martial law.

In March 1982 I confided to Fred that whatever we were doing it was not going to be a blow-by-blow reconstruction job. It would be irrelevant whether a particular meeting took place in Gdansk, Radom or Katowice, or who really said what. The last thing that would matter to us would be what kind or colour of car Jaruzelski was driving.

What, then, *were* we doing? We were going to address a particular question. It was a question to which the whole conflict between Solidarity and the Polish state was continually reduced: was freedom as defined by the free trade union Solidarity reconcilable with socialism as defined by the Eastern European Communist bloc?

I wrote to Fred, 'My position is that the two concepts cannot coexist and are irreconcilable in an absolute sense, in the sense understood by a logician or a mathematician: a mathematician knows that certain things cannot happen, not because no one has found out how to do them but because they are internally contradictory.'

The most familiar of these teasing impossibilities is the impossibility of turning a circle into a square with the same area.

Another question remained: who was the fallible narrator? On-camera and off-camera he expressed opinions, purported to know the facts, and evidently had a thesis about freedom and socialism. In an obvious sense he was myself. On the first page of the script I put an asterisk next to 'Narrator' and at the bottom of the page explained 'The author'. For the next year or more I was inside the film as well as outside it, until I was vetoed by the Americans. But that is to get ahead of the story.

Fred began his pilgrimage to find a director and the money. The money was harder. As time went on, the first director went off to do something for the BBC, the second for ITV, the third to make a feature film, the fourth to make an American TV block-buster. The first director returned, but now a year had gone by, *Squaring the Circle* had American strings and the Americans didn't want him. The director they did want, director number five, preferred to do something else, and directors number six and number seven seemed interested for a while but dropped out.

Our director, as it turned out, was worth waiting for. This was Mike Hodges.

At various times, *Squaring the Circle* was going to be filmed on location in Hamburg, Liverpool, Helsinki or, alternatively, when we seemed to have missed the snow in Hamburg, Liverpool and even Helsinki, on numberless reconstructions in different studios. It was going to have lots of ambience or it was going to be enclosed in a series of rooms: it was going to be as immaculate as a Hollywood movie or as exciting as newsreel shot from the hip; it was going to star international names or it was going to be made with totally unknown actors.

Mike brought in the designer, Voytek, who is Polish, and in a very short time they took over one of the sound stages at Pinewood, where they built a structure of steel gantries squaring off a huge red circular carpet on a steel floor. To this they added background flats and a few large movable pieces, such as a Polish eagle and a huge bust of Lenin. This space served as an airport, a street, a dockyard, the Polish parliament, the meeting rooms of the Politburo and Solidarity, and anywhere else we needed.

The result perfectly expressed the qualified reality which I had been worrying about creating since starting to write.

Next Mike politely declined the international stars and took on board Bernard Hill, Alec McCowen, Roy Kinnear, Frank Middlemass, John Woodvine and a whole gang of first-rate British actors.

Best of all, Mike immediately identified himself with the self-sceptical tone of the 'documentary' and understood why the narrator and the author had fused together. Other directors had been worried that the quirky bits of the script merely disturbed the straightforward bits, and wondered whether we might not be better off without them. Mike's reaction was to ask for more quirky bits. A man after my own heart.

After a year of stop and go I had frozen the text, the third draft, until we *really* had a director. Now I did another draft, adding a character who in different guises periodically interrupted and corrected the narrator. Mike suggested that this character ought to be five different characters. He also championed one of my earliest notions, that a key meeting between Walesa, Jaruzelski and Archbishop Glemp, of which almost nothing was known, should be seen in perhaps three different versions. Altogether, and at long last, the film was in the hands of someone who knew what he wanted, and my enthusiasm for it, which had almost died, was suddenly alive again.

Right at the beginning Fred had taken the project to Television South, who took it over along with what was then thought to be half the bill, £300,000. TVS brought in another independent producer, Peter Snell, with more investment but the budget crept upwards. The British company went to America looking for a pre-sale deal with NBC, CBS or perhaps one of the large commercial sponsors like Xerox, who might have £400,000 to invest in our little show. In the end, *Squaring the Circle* cost £1,264,661. By that time everything was in dollars, $800,000 of which were down to Metromedia.

Metromedia, based in Los Angeles, is a small giant compared to the big three networks in the United States but it has seven metropolitan TV stations of its own, covering a quarter of the viewing public of the entire country, and has its faith and its money in game shows, talk shows and main-chance series. All these have to be sold to the other 75 per cent of the viewing public through advertising sponsors. It was these people, these sellers of razor blades and cat food, who become Metromedia's scapegoats during the months to come. At the Pinewood end of the Metromedia chain of command there was Steve, who had to deal with Bruce, who had to deal with Dale, who had to deal with Chuck, who had to deal with Bob, and way beyond Bob, somewhere at the top of the mountain, there was the mysterious figure of Mr Kluge, remote as Buddha . . . and once, when the usual wrangle brought the usual response that there was no point in appealing to the personal taste (or at least the higher authority) of, successively, Bruce, Dale, Chuck and Bob because *they* were at the mercy of the advertisers (who were in thrall to the viewing millions), I desperately suggested an appeal to Mr Kluge. Steve realized he was dealing with a virgin. The idea that Mr Kluge, invisible in the stratosphere of high finance, would read a script . . . meet a writer. . . .

Anyway, by the early summer of 1983 TVS had made a pre-sale deal with Metromedia and it seemed that *Squaring the Circle*, which had not quite been made on previous occasions, was going to be made after all. For this, evidently, we had to thank Steve Schlow. Steve had liked the script and had undertaken to persuade Bruce, and so on. The first time I met Steve he remarked in a friendly way that I shouldn't think of him as the ugly American. In a equally friendly way I told him that the ugly American was his allotted role and there was nothing he could do about it.

The first sign of ugliness concerned the matter of the narrator. Steve, or rather not Steve, nor Bruce, nor Dale, nor Chuck, nor Bob but in fact the dreaded advertisers, and not actually the advertisers but the dreaded public, felt that the narrator should be an American, a *famous* American, with whom the (American) public could identify. I explained that, unfortunately, the internal logic of the script now required the narrator and the author to be the same person. The narrator, after all, was purporting to express a personal opinion. Whose opinion would Jason Robards be expressing? (Likewise Jack Lemmon, Charlton Heston, Donald Sutherland and other names which came down from the lower slopes of the mountain.) I assumed that my argument would carry the day, which was an assumption at least as naive as the idea that Mr Kluge read scripts. As it turned out, the script that Fred had sent to Metromedia did not contain my asterisk. This script, dated May 1983, had been given a glossy cover on which was depicted a bayonet spearing the word 'Solidarnosc', which was bleeding down the page. I liked the cover but never bothered to check the contents and so was unaware of the missing asterisk and the missing footnote saying 'The author'. Weeks later I lent my copy to a friend who didn't think much of it but liked one particular scene which he described to me. The scene was not familiar. On checking, I discovered that it had been added, and there were significant changes on seven pages. Evidently I was in the hands of desperate men.

In August I happened to be in Los Angeles and with the encouragement of the British team I made an appointment with the awesome Bruce. We had breakfast in the Polo Lounge of the Beverly Hills Hotel (where else?). Bruce turned out to be as puzzled by me as I was by him, because the narrator was not negotiable and never had been; the Famous American was an absolute condition of the deal and Bruce thought that everybody in England already knew that.

I conceded the narrator, and not withstanding the admirable Richard Crenna, who *played* him much better than I could have ever *been* him, I still regret it. What was supposed to have been a kind of personal dramatized essay turned into a kind of play about an unexplained American in Poland. Later I was asked to fix up the script to explain what this American was doing there, but since I had no idea, I did nothing.

Meanwhile (September 1983) things had progressed satisfactorily. Encouraged by Mike I had written the quirky version of the script and Steve was still with us. It was known and accepted that the American version would have to contain seven commercial breaks and consequently would be about nine minutes shorter than the British version.

It should be said that throughout all these adventures TVS, in the person of James Gatward, stayed with us too, and never complained when the script which they had originally accepted was whipped away and replaced by the quirkier one.

Shooting began in October. Steve moved to England for the duration. He and Fred, separately or together, were often on the set. It seemed reasonable that Steve should be curious to see what was happening to Metromedia's $800,000, but his precise status on the project remained unclear, with ultimately disastrous results. As far as Mike Hodges and I were concerned, we were employed by TVS to make a film for Channel 4, and Metromedia had paid for the right to show the result in the United States. This turned out to be the greatest naivety of all, as the printed credits make clear.

One day Mike and I decided that the scene between Walesa, Jaruzelski and Archbishop Glemp seemed a bit stodgy and so overnight I rewrote it as a card game. Steve expressed doubts. Perhaps it would be best to film the scene both ways? But the schedule was tight, and after all we were not working for Metromedia, we were working for TVS. The penny should have dropped with the sound of 800,000 silver dollars, but we never heard it. Mike brought the film in triumphantly in five weeks, and on 26 January 1984 there was a message from Dale to TVS: 'The version which you have accepted for the British market is not a film which we feel can successfully compete for advertiser support or for viewers. . . . This is not simply a matter of reviewing certain scenes in order to cut the film to our required ninety-five minutes.'

It became rapidly clear that Metromedia had bought not merely the right to show the film but the right to alter it in any way they liked.

Mike's relationship with Steve, which had hardly existed, disintegrated completely. In due course Steve returned from California with a video tape of *Squaring the Circle* which he had cut and rearranged, losing the overall shape of the film and dispensing with the five characters who served the crucial purpose of distancing the film from the conventional kind of docudrama which (falsely) purports to reconstruct history. The final scene, which was the book-end for the first scene, had been cut. There was an attempt to put something of Walesa at the very beginning of the film, although the script had carefully saved the entrance of Walesa for a climactic moment well into the story. And the card game had been chopped to bits.

Steve did not invite Mike to view the tape. 'What's the point?' he said. 'Mike would storm out of the room within five minutes.'

Nevertheless I phoned Mike to tell him of the viewing and, when he didn't show up, suggested that Steve should get in touch with him. Steve didn't do that either and this was the last straw. Steve had already blotted his copybook by running the unfinished film without Mike's permission, a serious breach of protocol. Mike had been threatening to take his name off the American version and now he did so. I gathered that he wasn't entirely pleased by my having gone so far as to view the American tape in those circumstances, but I saw my position as being rather different from his because theoretically I still owed my services to Metromedia since it had been agreed that I would modify the narration in whatever way was necessary to tidy up the nine-minute cuts. Having seen the tape, I told Steve that not only had he spoiled the film, he had made nonsense of some of it, and in my opinion had not even succeeded in ending up with something which stood a better chance with the game-show public. This cut no ice (it wasn't *Steve* who was doing this, or Bruce, or Dale, or Chuck, or Bob, it was those advertisers again). So I, too, took my name off the American version.

Thus the horse-trading began. On the telephone I listed my half-dozen major demands. Did I mean, Steve asked, that if these things were done I would put my name back on the film? I told him that it would mean that we would still have something to talk about. He said he would ask California. California started to relent. Walesa disappeared from the top of the film, the last scene was restored, the card game was put back into its proper form, and a number of other things were put right. I thought I was doing rather well and reported these successes to Mike, who, however, took a different view which he expressed with much more kindness than he must have been feeling towards me. The way he saw it, Metromedia were messing about with our film and I was helping them. The way I saw it, Metromedia had the legal right to do their worst and I was trying to ameliorate it. The closer I got the American film back to where we wanted it, and it was never close enough, the more it proved to Mike that if only I had held firm Metromedia would have knuckled under frame for frame. Thus, the more battles I won, the more evident my error.

I kept winning. By April the only large battle remaining was one which had looked lost from the beginning, the inclusion or exclusion of the five characters, the 'witnesses', who spoke to the narrator. Once more in Los Angeles, I made my first visit to the Metromedia building which, as is the way with important American companies, seemed to be a museum of modern art with space let out for business. The art itself had apparently been chosen to balance the image of Metromedia's products and, if screened, would not have stood an earthly of competing successfully for advertiser support. Some of it was outside, and the largest piece looked as if part of Voytek's set had crashed into the roof. Here I met an ally in Richard Crenna. Richard said that without the witnesses in the script he would never have accepted the part. The witnesses brought the narrator into the film and without them *Squaring the Circle* would not be the film he had agreed to make. By the time we left the building, the only outstanding question seemed to be whether we would use the witnesses as originally filmed or save something of the idea by keeping the most important witness and reshooting some extra bits with Crenna and the First Witness alone. (We did the latter.) In England I reported progress to Mike. He was as magnanimous as he could be. He didn't think I was malicious, merely naive.

It is a distressing situation which alters itself and alters back again like one of those optical illusions drawn to amuse children. Sometimes my view is Mike's view, that Metromedia knew what they were getting into (give or take a card game) and one should have no further truck with the devil. But most times the overriding thought is that it's more important to save what can be saved than to let them take the hindmost.

But on what authority have I acted? Authorship. This is tricky. On one occasion during these negotiations, Steve demonstrated to me that because of the insertion of a commercial break where none existed in the British film, two of the scenes worked better when they were transposed. As the author of the pages in question I felt I had the right to agree or disagree, and I agreed. But, of course, the pages were no longer pages but bits of film, which, as everyone knows, is a director's medium.

Months ago when the credit titles were being planned Mike turned down the offer of 'A Mike Hodges film' and with characteristic kindness towards me suggested instead 'A film by Mike Hodges and Tom Stoppard'. That film, as transmitted on Channel 4 in May 1984, in the one which is closest to the present text.

*    *    *

*Every Good Boy Deserves Favour* is the title of a work of which the text is only a part. The subtitle, 'A Play for Actors and Orchestra', hardly indicates the extent to which the effectiveness of the whole depends on the music composed by André Previn. And it is to him that the work owes its existence.

As the principal conductor of the London Symphony Orchestra, Mr Previn invited me in 1974 to write something which had the need of a live full-size orchestra on stage. Invitations don't come much rarer than that, and I jumped at the chance. It turned out to be the fastest move I made on the project for the next eighteen months.

Usually, and preferably, a play originates in the author's wish to write about some particular thing. The form of the play then follows from the requirements of the subject. This time I found myself trying to make the subject follow from the requirements of the form. Mr Previn and I agreed early on that we would try to go beyond a mere recitation for the concert platform, and also that we were not writing a piece for singers. In short, it was going to be a real play, to be performed in conjunction with, and bound up with, a symphony orchestra. As far as we knew nobody had tried to do anything like that before; which, again, is not the preferred reason for starting a play, though I confess it weighed with me.

Having been given *carte blanche*, for a long time the only firm decision I was able to make was that the play would have to be in some way *about* an orchestra. For what play could escape *folie de grandeur* if it came with a hundred musicians in attendance but outside the action? And while it is next to impossible to 'justify' an orchestra, it is a simple matter to make it essential. Accordingly, I started off with a millionaire who owned one.

My difficulty in trying to make the cart pull the horse was aggravated by the fact that I knew nothing about orchestras and very little about 'serious' music. I was in the position of a man who, never having read anything but whodunnits, finds himself writing a one-man show about Lord Byron on a *carte blanche* from an actor with a club foot. My qualifications for writing about an orchestra amounted to a spell as a triangle-player in a kindergarten percussion band. I informed my collaborator that the play was going to be about a millionaire triangle-player with his own orchestra.

This basic implausibility bred others, and at the point where the whimsical edifice was about to collapse I tried to save it by making the orchestra a mere delusion of the millionaire's brain. Once the orchestra became an imaginary orchestra, there was no need for the millionaire to be a millionaire either. I changed tack: the play would be about a lunatic triangle-player who thought he had an orchestra.

By this time the first deadline had been missed and I was making heavy weather. I had no genuine reason for writing about an orchestra, or a lunatic, and thus had nothing to write. Music and triangles led me into a punning diversion based on Euclid's axioms, but it didn't belong anywhere, and I was ready to call my own bluff.

This is where matters stood when in April 1976 I met Victor Fainberg. For some months previously I had been reading books and articles by and about the Russian dissidents, intending to use the material for a television play, and so I knew that Mr Fainberg had been one of a group of people arrested in Red Square in August 1968 during a peaceful demonstration against the Warsaw Pact invasion of Czechoslovakia. He had been pronounced insane – a not unusual fate for perfectly sane opponents of Soviet tyranny – and in 1974 he had emerged into exile from five years in the Soviet prison-hospital system. He had written about his experiences in the magazine *Index on Censorship*, an invaluable, politically disinterested monitor of political repression the world over. For Mr Fainberg freedom was, and is, mainly the freedom to double his efforts on behalf of colleagues left behind. His main concern when I met him was to secure the release of Vladimir Bukovsky, himself a victim of the abuse of psychiatry in the USSR, whose revelations about that abuse had got him sentenced to consecutive terms of prison, labour camp and internal exile amounting to twelve years.

Exceptional courage is a quality drawn from certain people in exceptional conditions. Although British society is not free of abuses, we are not used to meeting courage because conditions do not demand it. (I am not thinking of the courage with which people face, say, an illness or a bereavement.) Mr Fainberg's single-mindedness, his energy (drawing more on anger than on pity) and his willingness to make a nuisance of himself outside and inside the walls of any institution, friend or foe, which bore upon his cause, prompted the thought that his captors must have been quite pleased to get rid of him. He was not a man to be broken or silenced; an insistent, discordant note, one might say, in an orchestrated society.

I don't recall that I consciously made the metaphor, but very soon I was able to tell Mr Previn, definitively, that the lunatic triangle-player who thought he had an orchestra was now sharing a cell with a political prisoner. I had something to write about, and in a few weeks the play was finished.

Not that the prisoner, Alexander, is Victor or anyone else. But the speech in which he describes the treatment he received in the Leningrad Special Psychiatric Hospital is taken from the article in *Index*,* and there are other borrowings from life, such as the doctor's comment, 'Your opinions are your symptoms.' Victor Fainberg in his own identity makes an appearance in the text as one of the group 'M to S' in the speech where Alexander identifies people by letters of the alphabet.

The off-stage hero of *Every Good Boy Deserves Favour*, referred to as 'my friend C', is Vladimir Bukovsky. The Bukovsky campaign, which was supported by many people in several countries, achieved its object in December 1976, when he was taken from prison and sent to the West. In June while we were rehearsing I met Mr Bukovsky in London and invited him to call round at the Royal Shakespeare Company's rehearsal rooms in Covent Garden. He came and stayed to watch for an hour or two. He was diffident, friendly, and helpful on points of detail in the production, but his presence was disturbing. For people working on a piece of theatre, terra firma is a self-

---

*Index on Censorship*, vol. 4, no. 2, published by a non-profit-making company, Writers and Scholars International, 39c Highbury Place, London N5.

contained world even while it mimics the real one. That is the necessary condition of making theatre, and it is also our luxury. There was a sense of worlds colliding. I began to feel embarrassed. One of the actors seized up in the middle of a speech touching on the experiences of our visitor, and found it impossible to continue. But the incident was not fatal. The effect wore off, and, on the night, *Every Good Boy Deserves Favour* had recovered its nerve and its own reality.

\*     \*     \*

The television play which I had hoped to write from the Russian material still had to be written. At least, I had promised myself that I would write a television play to mark Amnesty International's 'Prisoner of Conscience Year' (1977), and I had promised the BBC that I would come up with something by 31 December 1976. On that day I had nothing to show, nothing begun and nothing in mind.

On 6 January in Prague three men, a playwright, an actor and a journalist, were arrested in the act of attempting to deliver a document to their own Government. This document turned out to be a request that the Government should implement its own laws. It pointed out that the Czechoslovak people had been deprived of rights guaranteed by an agreement made between nations at Helsinki, and that anyone who tried to claim these rights was victimized by the Government which had put its name to the agreement. The document, initially signed by 241 people, was headed 'Charter 77'.

I had had ill-formed and unformed thoughts of writing about Czechoslovakia for a year or two. Moreover, I had been strongly drawn to the work and personality of the arrested playwright, Vaclav Havel. Thus it would be natural to expect that the setting and subject matter of *Professional Foul* declared themselves as soon as the Charter story broke, but in fact I was still sifting through a mass of Amnesty International documents about Russia, and when a friend invited me to keep him company on a week's visit to Moscow and Leningrad, I went hoping that the trip would unlock the play.

Perhaps predictably, the trip made the play much more difficult, since it brought me too close to the situation to leave me with any desire to trick it out with 'character', 'dramatic shape', 'dénouement', and so on, but not close enough to enable me to write about it from the inside. Instead, the trip to Russia unlocked a play about Czechoslovakia: there was an Archimedean footing, somewhere between involvement and detachment, which offered a point of leverage. By the beginning of March the general scheme of *Professional Foul* had been worked out, and after that the play was written very quickly, the first draft in about three weeks.

Meanwhile, Vaclav Havel was in gaol, on charges devised to dissociate his arrest from his activities as a spokesman for Charter 77. After four and a half months he was released, pending his trial; which took place while this Introduction was being written. For 'attempting to damage the name of the State abroad', Mr Havel was sentenced to fourteen months, suspended for two years.*

He would be the first to object that in mentioning his name only, I am putting undue emphasis on his part in the Czechoslovakian human rights movement. Others have gone to gaol, and many more have been victimized. This is true. But I have in mind not just the Chartist but the author of *The Garden Party*, *The Memorandum*, *The Audience* and other plays. It is to a fellow writer that I dedicate *Professional Foul* in admiration.

*1984.

# SQUARING THE CIRCLE
## Poland 1980–1

### A Film for Television

## Characters

NARRATOR
LEONID BREZHNEV
EDWARD GIEREK
BREZHNEV'S AIDE
BABIUCH
KANIA
SZYDLAK
WOJCIECH JARUZELSKI
BARCIKOWSKI
JAGIELSKI
FINANSKY
FIRST ELECTRICIAN
SECOND ELECTRICIAN
MACIEJ SZCZEPANSKI
JACEK KURON
GEREMEK
GIEREK'S SECRETARY
GERMAN BANKER
AMERICAN BANKER
SWISS BANKER
GIRL
CARDINAL WYSZYNSKI
STEFAN OLSZOWSKI
LECH WALESA
PRISONER

WALESA CHILDREN
DANUTA WALESA
MAZOWIECKI
MODZELEWSKI
MARIAN JURCZYK
ANDRZEJ GWIAZDA
JAN RULEWSKI
BUJAK
BOGDAN LIS
JUDGE
GANG MEMBER
PRIEST
PUBLIC PROSECUTOR
SOVIET AMBASSADOR
GERMAN SPOKESMAN
MARSHAL KULIKOV
WORKER
PARTY OFFICIAL
MIECZYSLAW RAKOWSKI
DOCTOR
PARTY MAN
MINER
KATOWICE MAN
JARUZELSKI'S SECRETARY
ARCHBISHOP JOSEPH GLEMP

WITNESSES, AIDES, SECRETARIES, POLICEMEN, GUARDS, MILITARY
OFFICERS, JOURNALISTS, PHOTOGRAPHERS, WORKERS, PRIESTS, etc.

*Squaring the Circle* was first transmitted in May 1984 by TVS. The cast included:

| | |
|---|---|
| NARRATOR | Richard Crenna |
| LEONID BREZHNEV | Frank Middlemass |
| EDWARD GIEREK | John Woodvine |
| BABIUCH | John Bluthal |
| KANIA | Roy Kinnear |
| WOJCIECH JARUZELSKI | Richard Kane |
| JACEK KURON | Don Henderson |
| LECH WALESA | Bernard Hill |
| MARIAN JURCZYK | John Rogan |
| ANDRZEJ GWIAZDA | Jonathan Adams |
| JAN RULEWSKI | Tom Wilkinson |
| MIECZYSLAW RAKOWSKI | Alec McCowen |
| | |
| *Director* | Mike Hodges |
| *Production Designer* | Voytek |
| *Director of Photography* | Michael Garfath |

# Part One: The First Secretary

1. EXT. SEA SHORE. SUMMER DAY

*Empty beach. Sea. Sky.*

*With the mention of his name we find* EDWARD GIEREK, *a middle-aged man in a suit, overcoat, hat and lace-up shoes, walking along by the sea.*

NARRATOR: (*Voice over*) Towards the end of July 1980 Edward
Gierek, First Secretary of the Polish United Workers'
Party, which is to say the boss of Communist Poland, left
Warsaw for his annual holiday in the Soviet Union by the
Black Sea. There he met . . .

(BREZHNEV, *similarly dressed, is walking towards* GIEREK.)

. . . Leonid Brezhnev, First Secretary of the Communist
party of the USSR.

(*The two men meet and grasp each other's shoulders and kiss
each other on both cheeks.*)

In an atmosphere of cordiality and complete mutual
understanding the two leaders had a frank exchange of
views.

BREZHNEV: Comrade! As your friends and allies in the progress
towards the inevitable triumph of Marxist-Leninism, we are
concerned, deeply concerned, by recent departures from
Leninist norms by Polish workers manipulated by a
revisionist element of the Polish intelligentsia!

GIEREK: Comrade First Secretary! As your friends and allies in
the proletariat's struggle against international
capitalism . . .

(GIEREK *evidently continues in the same vein.*)

NARRATOR: (*Voice over*) That isn't them, of course –

(*Close up on the* NARRATOR, *in the same location.*)

(*To camera*) – and this isn't the Black Sea. Everything is true
except the words and the pictures. If there was a beach,

27

Brezhnev and Gierek probably didn't talk on it, and if they did, they probably wouldn't have been wearing, on a beach in July, those hats and coats and lace-up shoes which you get for being a Communist leader. They were after all . . .

2. EXT. SEASIDE. SUMMER DAY

NARRATOR: (*Voice over*) . . . supposed to be on holiday.
(*There are gay umbrellas and cool brightly coloured drinks to hand. Everything in fact is highly coloured.* BREZHNEV *and* GIEREK *are now wearing brightly coloured Hawaiian shirts and slacks. They wear sunglasses. They drink from pink drinks with little purple paper umbrellas sticking out of them.* BREZHNEV, *however, is attended by two or three* AIDES *who are dressed in dark suits. The one who is going to speak wears a suit and is carrying a file of papers ostentatiously marked* Poland.)
And even if you got the look of it right, they probably didn't talk like a *Pravda* editorial, because if you're the boss of the Communist Party of the Soviet Union and if you've got twenty armoured divisions in East Germany and your supply lines have to go across Poland and the Polish railway workers are on strike, you don't say that you are deeply concerned about departures from Leninist norms, you probably say –

BREZHNEV: (*Shouting like a gangster*) What the hell is going on with you guys? Who's running the country? You or the engine drivers? Your work force has got you by the short hairs because you're up to your neck in hock to German bankers, American bankers, Swiss bankers – you're in hock to *us* to the tune of . . . (*glances at the* AIDE *for aid*) . . . is it millions or billions. . . ?
(*The* AIDE *panics for a second, shuffling and dropping his papers, but rises to the occasion.*)

AIDE: Zillions.

BREZHNEV: (*Triumphantly shouts*) Zillions of roubles!

AIDE: Zlotys.

BREZHNEV: (*Rounding on him*) You shut up!

3. EXT. SEASIDE. SUMMER DAY

NARRATOR: (*To camera*) Who knows?

All the same, there was something going on which remains true even when the words and the pictures are mostly made up. Between August 1980 and December 1981 an attempt was made in Poland to put together two ideas which wouldn't fit, the idea of freedom as it is understood in the West, and the idea of socialism as it is understood in the Soviet empire. The attempt failed because it was impossible, in the same sense as it is impossible in geometry to turn a circle into a square with the same area – not because no one has found out how to do it, but because there is no way in which it can be done. What happened in Poland was that a number of people tried for sixteen months to change the shape of the system without changing the area covered by the original shape. They failed.

4. EXT. AIRFIELD. NIGHT

*So* EDWARD GIEREK *is met by Prime Minister* BABIUCH. *They grasp each other's shoulders and kiss each other on the cheek.*

NARRATOR: (*Voice over*) Edward Gierek came home from the Black Sea on August 15th.

BABIUCH: Welcome home, Comrade. I'm sorry you had to cut short your holiday.

(*But* GIEREK *is immediately concerned with part of his holiday luggage which is being taken off the plane by a uniformed* MINION. *The item is a large beach bag out of which protrudes a snorkel and a ridiculous straw hat. The* MINION *jostles the bag which clinks dangerously.*)

GIEREK: Careful with that . . .

(GIEREK *takes the bag from the* MINION. GIEREK *and* BABIUCH *wait for the car which is to take them away.*)

BABIUCH: Comrade Kania has been to Gdansk.

GIEREK: Why?

BABIUCH: Why? Because the Lenin shipyard in Gdansk is at a complete standstill. The Party Secretary up there telephoned yesterday in a panic.

GIEREK: I know all that. Do we have to have a member of the Politburo rushing to the scene whenever there's a disruption of working norms?

BABIUCH: You sent Jagielski to settle the railway strike.

GIEREK: The railway disruption of working norms was different.

BABIUCH: Kania says this one is different.

GIEREK: How much are they asking for?

BABIUCH: Two thousand a month, but it's not the money that worries us.

GIEREK: It should. It's the money we haven't got.

(*Car pulls in front. The car door is being held open for them.*)

BABIUCH: After you, Comrade First Secretary.

GIEREK: Thank you, Comrade Prime Minister.

(BABIUCH *takes* GIEREK's *bag for him.*)

BABIUCH: Allow me . . .

(GIEREK *gets into the car followed by* BABIUCH *and the beach bag.*)


### 5. INT. THE CAR. NIGHT

GIEREK *and* BABIUCH *in the back seat.* GIEREK *takes the bag from* BABIUCH *and searches about in it during the narration.*

NARRATOR: (*Voice over*) The Prime Minister is, of course, the head of the government. Today, and for several days to come his name is Mr Babiuch. Apart from having a prime minister, Poland has elections, a parliament and a head of state, much like Britain or France or America.

(GIEREK *finds what he has been looking for in the bag – which he hands to* BABIUCH, *who is suitably grateful.*)

GIEREK: I've brought you some caviar.


### 6. EXT. PARTY HEADQUARTERS. NIGHT

*The car draws up.* GIEREK *and* BABIUCH *get out of the car and enter the building. The door is opened by a doorman. This person is going to pop up again in various guises throughout the film, so for simplicity's sake he will henceforth be referred to as the* WITNESS. *The* NARRATOR *enters the frame.*

NARRATOR: (*To camera*) This is where it all gets different from bourgeois Western democracy. In the East, they have the window dressing but the shop is run by the Party. Through nominees and controlled elections the Party dominates parliament and manages the machinery of the state, and thus is in a position to fulfil its sacred trust of defending the interests of the working people . . .

7. INT. PARTY HEADQUARTERS. NIGHT

BABIUCH *is carrying* GIEREK's *bag.* GIEREK *sees* KANIA *coming up behind, and pauses to fish about in the bag, so that he is able to greet* KANIA *with another jar of caviar.*

NARRATOR: (*Voice over*) . . . with caviar and limousines.

8. EXT. PARTY HEADQUARTERS. NIGHT

*The* NARRATOR *has just finished addressing the camera and is interrupted by the* WITNESS.

WITNESS: A cheap shot, in my opinion. These people are not doormen. These are people with big responsibilities.

NARRATOR: Just making an observation.

WITNESS: It's not a factor. I never saw the President of France arrive anywhere on a bicycle eating a salami sandwich.

NARRATOR: Excuse me.

(*To camera*) It works like this. The Party Congress, about 2,000 delegates who meet every five years not counting emergencies, elects a Central Committee of about 200 members who meet as and when to supervise Party policy. To implement that policy the Central Committee elects . . .

9. INT. POLITBURO MEETING. NIGHT

NARRATOR: (*Voice over*) . . . the Political Bureau.

(*There are about a dozen members of the Politburo, now seen placing themselves at a large table. They include* GIEREK, BABIUCH, KANIA, SZYDLAK, JARUZELSKI, BARCIKOWSKI, JAGIELSKI *and* FINANSKY. ('Finansky' *is an invented name to allow two different finance ministers to be represented in one character.*))

This is not a meeting of the Government. This is the Politburo.

(GIEREK *is the chairman. He invites* KANIA *to begin.*)

GIEREK: Comrade Kania. . . ?

KANIA: At Gdansk in the Lenin shipyard they demand . . . number one, a wage increase of 2,000 zlotys a month. Number two, reinstatement of sacked trouble-makers. Number three, family allowances increased to the same level enjoyed by police and security forces. Number four, earlier retirement. Number five, a monument outside the main gate . . .

GIEREK: A monument?

KANIA: Yes. To the dead of 1970. The strike spokesman is
obsessed with putting up a monument. He was in the
shipyard in Gdansk in 1970. He's been arrested more than
once for holding demonstrations outside the gate on the
anniversary . . . Actually, he's been arrested about a
hundred times for one thing or another. The shipyard
director tried to settle for a plaque in the dining hall but he
insists on a monument, forty metres high.

GIEREK: Is he mad?

SZYDLAK: That's an idea . . .

KANIA: (*To* SZYDLAK) No.

GIEREK: Who is he?

KANIA: Walesa. You've met him.

GIEREK: When?

KANIA: Ten years ago. After the 1970 riots. You went to talk to
the workers in the Baltic ports –

GIEREK: Yes.

KANIA: In Gdansk there was a three-man delegation. Walesa was
one of them. Moustache. He didn't speak. You remember
him?

GIEREK: No.

KANIA: Well, I think they'd settle for the money and the
reinstatements. Enough of them would, anyway.

(GIEREK *looks towards* FINANSKY.)

FINANSKY: There is already more money than there are goods to
spend it on. The situation is inflationary, and would be
more so if we did not keep food cheap artificially. The
farmer buys bread to feed the pigs because it is cheaper
than the wheat he sells to us. Then we buy the pigs for 130
zlotys per kilo and we sell the butcher's pork for 70 zlotys.
Such subsidies are costing us 3 billion zlotys a year. As a
matter of fact the same money would pay our interest to
Western bankers this year.

GIEREK: (*To* KANIA) We cannot give way on the money. It buys
nothing.

KANIA: It buys time.

GIEREK: Are you an economist?

32

KANIA: I have been to Gdansk.

GIEREK: If we give way on the money in Gdansk, Gdynia will demand the same. Then Szczecin. It'll spread everywhere.

KANIA: So will the strike if we don't stop it.

SZYDLAK: Send in the police, the state security . . .

KANIA: There's no public disorder.

SZYDLAK: A strike is a public disorder. In fact it's illegal. If the police can't handle it send in the army.

(*The members turn generally towards* JARUZELSKI, *who is in general's uniform.*)

JARUZELSKI: To do what? I said in 1970 that I wouldn't order Polish soldiers to shoot Polish workers.

SZYDLAK: But they did shoot. The army and the police. And the strikers went back to work.

JARUZELSKI: Not all of them.

SZYDLAK: All of them.

JARUZELSKI: Not the ones who were dead.

GIEREK: The Minister of Defence is quite right. We must not repeat December 1970. And if you remember, the men in the shipyards did not go back to work until I went to talk to them. January '71. The bloodstains were still on the streets. I had been First Secretary for one month. The pickets at the gate didn't recognize me. I had to tell them who I was. It's not so surprising. When did the Party leader ever come to debate with the workers face to face on their own ground? And we talked. I told them how I had worked in the mines in Belgium and France. With these hands. I said to them, help us, help *me*, I'm a worker too. We can start again. I told them there was going to be a new spirit. A new Poland. A rich Poland. But the poison got back into the system. (*Helplessly*) What does one do. . . ?

KANIA: We've cut the phone lines from Gdansk.

GIEREK: No – it's time to be frank. We have to tell the country what's going on.

JARUZELSKI: Everybody listens to the foreign radio stations – they know what's going on.

GIEREK: If they know, we can afford to be frank. We must explain the shortages . . . the danger of inflation . . . we must appeal to patriotism and common sense.

BABIUCH: (*Dubiously*) Do you really think. . . ?

GIEREK: We must, of course, accept some of the blame. On the radio and television, tonight.

BABIUCH: Will you do it?

GIEREK: Me? No, you're the Prime Minister.


IO. THE SAME. NIGHT

*In other words, the Politburo meeting continues into the night, now without* BABIUCH *. . . who is, however, present and talking, on a television set which the rest of the Politburo are watching. The formality of the meeting has disintegrated. Ties are loosened, cups and glasses are littered about. The cut is to* BABIUCH *on the television but his speech is mostly audible wallpaper for the camera's travel.*

BABIUCH: It has to be admitted that in the past we have not always managed to deal efficiently with economic difficulties. The public has not been given sufficient information about our troubles, about the state of the economy and the growing problems as and when they occurred. We have not prepared ourselves sufficiently for the difficult times which we should have seen as inevitable. Even today, not everyone realizes what our country's economic situation is like. To put it bluntly, our country's indebtedness has reached a point which must not on any account be overstepped. We have been living and developing on credit. Stopping work not only harms the national economy, it also turns against the working class and working people in general, damaging their vital interests. The opponents of People's Poland are trying to use the atmosphere of tension and emotion for their own political ends, putting forward slogans and suggestions which have nothing in common with the aspirations of the working class.

(*During this*:)

KANIA: (*To* GIEREK) What do we do if it doesn't work?

GIEREK: We could try another prime minister.

KANIA: Seriously, we'll have to make them an offer.

GIEREK: How much?

KANIA: Fifteen hundred, and the reinstatement of trouble-makers, and the monument.

GIEREK: Will they settle?

KANIA: Yes.

GIEREK: All right. I'm going home. I don't want to be called except in an emergency. (*Points at* BABIUCH *on the television.*) This is for Comrade Brezhnev.

BABIUCH: (*On television*) The world is watching us, wondering how we can manage in these difficult moments . . .


11. INT. CAFE. NIGHT

*A café in Poland. There is a television set.* BABIUCH *is continuing to speak.*

BABIUCH: (*On television*) We have reliable allies who also worry about our troubles and believe that we will be able to overcome them ourselves. They wish us success from the bottom of their hearts.

(*Among the people in the café are the* NARRATOR *and the* WITNESS.)

NARRATOR: (*To camera*) Poland's reliable ally, her neighbour to the east, had been a watchful and threatening presence since 1945.

WITNESS: 1700.

(*The* NARRATOR *is about to protest.*)

All right, 1720 but no later. You won't understand Poland's attitude to Russia until you understand some Polish history. This won't take long.

NARRATOR: I hope not.

(*The* WITNESS *reaches over to an adjacent table for a basket of bread rolls which he tips over on to his own table. He pushes the bread rolls together in the middle of the table.*)

WITNESS: Nobody except the Poles remembers that for 300 years this was the biggest and freest country in Middle-Europe, spanning the continent from the Baltic almost to the Black Sea and reaching hundreds of miles east into modern Russia. Russia's greatness came *after* Poland's and was achieved at Poland's expense. During the eighteenth century, Poland came under Russian domination. This alarmed the other great powers, Austria and Prussia, so in 1772 Catherine the Great gave a bit of Poland to each of them to keep them quiet.

(*He detaches a couple of bread rolls, pushing them 'west', and a couple more 'south'.*)

This was the first of three partitions which were to
dismember the country by the end of the century. By the
standards of the time Poland had a liberal tradition,
squeezed now between three emperors. In 1793 Russia and
Prussia decided to cut Poland down to size.

(*He separates two bread rolls to the 'east' and two more to the
'west'. This leaves half a dozen bread rolls in the middle of the
table.*)

Poland, what was left of it, rebelled and in 1795 the three
power blocks finished the job.

(*He pushes two rolls to the 'west', two to the 'east' and two to
the 'south'. There are none left in the middle.*)

Poland disappeared. Of course there were still an awful lot
of Poles around and when Napoleon turned up to challenge
the great powers large numbers of them joined his armies.
The reward was the Duchy of Warsaw, 1807.

(*He places a single bread roll in the middle of the table.*)

It lasted as long as Napoleon lasted. And when the victors
met in Vienna to carve up the map, Russia got the prize.

(*He pushes the bread roll to the 'east'.*)

For a hundred years after that Poland was mainly an idea
kept alive by an underground at home and *emigrés* abroad.
The period of romantic exile.

NARRATOR: Oh yes, handsome young men in lace cuffs playing
the piano in Paris . . . I wondered.

WITNESS: They were waiting for a miracle. The miracle
happened in 1918 with the simultaneous collapse of the
Russian, Austrian and German empires. The victors met at
Versailles and put Poland back on the map.

(*He pushes two bread rolls from 'east', 'west' and 'south' into
the middle of the table.*)

In 1920 the old enemy, now known as Soviet Russia,
invaded and was repulsed. Poland survived until the Nazi–
Soviet pact in 1939.

(*He divides the six bread rolls and pushes them 'east' and
'west'.*)

The thieves fell out. Hitler lost. The allies met at Yalta to
carve up the map and Churchill and Roosevelt let Stalin

keep his prize.

(*He moves three bread rolls from 'west' to 'east'.*)

This is a true picture, except for the bread rolls. You don't get a basket of bread rolls put out on a café table in Poland. However, it is now possible to speak of 1945.

NARRATOR: (*To camera*) The first post-war Communist leader, Gomulka, was toppled in the Stalinist paranoia in 1948. Eight years of bad times growing steadily worse finally in 1956 touched off a huge working-class revolt which left eighty dead and brought Gomulka back as a reformer. Things got worse. This time it took fourteen years. Gomulka announced food price increases and touched off a workers' revolt in the Baltic ports in 1970. No one knows how many died, some say as many as 200. The massacre brought down Gomulka and elevated Edward Gierek.

### 12. INT. GIEREK'S ROOM

*Telephone ringing. As* GIEREK *moves through the frame:*

NARRATOR: (*Voice over*) Things got better and then the same. In 1976 Gierek announced food price increases. There were strikes. Gierek backed down. Things got better, then the same, then worse. Poland was going broke. In July 1980 Gierek announced food price increases. There were strikes. Railwaymen closed one of the main lines into Russia, or, to put it another way, one of the main lines into Poland. Gierek went to the Black Sea to meet Brezhnev. On August 14th the Lenin shipyard in Gdansk closed down. Gierek flew home the next day. The Politburo met. Prime Minister Babiuch went on television. Gierek went to the country, hoping that the crisis was over.

(GIEREK *answers the telephone. He listens for a few moments, annoyed.*)

GIEREK: (*Into phone*) You told me they would settle.

### 13. INT. PARTY HEADQUARTERS (POLITBURO). DAY

*The Politburo is meeting again.*

KANIA: It was in the balance. A majority at the shipyard voted to end the strike. They were swung back by a radical element.

SZYDLAK: Reactionary. You mean a reactionary element.

KANIA: The shipyard swung back to keep solidarity with the places still on strike.

GIEREK: (*Shakes his head impatiently.*) Solidarity.

KANIA: I said this one was not like the others. Now we're no longer dealing with a shipyard but a committee representing 150 plants and factories.

SZYDLAK: (*Furiously*) The scum want to set up an independent trade union! – They demand abolition of censorship – access to the media – This is not a strike. It's a bloody mutiny!

GIEREK: (*Sharply*) It's clear that the official trade unions have lost touch with the aspirations of their membership. You have forfeited their trust.

SZYDLAK: (*Surprised*) What kind of language is that?

GIEREK: You have let us down, Comrade! (*More calmly*) Independent unions are, of course, out of the question. But reform . . . yes. (*Looks directly at* SZYDLAK) A reform of the official unions. (*To* KANIA) Now I will have to talk to them.

KANIA: Do you want me to come with you?

GIEREK: No – on TV. (*To* BABIUCH) My turn.


14. INT. TELEVISION STUDIO

GIEREK *speaks to a single television camera. He is apparently in his office, sitting at a desk, the office bookcase behind him.*

GIEREK: I would like to say as frankly as I can that we are aware that quite apart from many objective factors, mistakes in economic policy have played an important part . . . We understand the working people's tiredness and impatience with the troubles of everyday life, the shortages, the queues, the rise in the cost of living . . .

(*Our camera has tilted slowly up, to find two* ELECTRICIANS *standing on a gantry, looking down on* GIEREK.)

FIRST ELECTRICIAN: I think I've seen this before . . .

SECOND ELECTRICIAN: Typical bloody August . . . nothing but repeats.

(*We cut to a different angle of* GIEREK *talking to the television camera. We see his image on a monitor, being watched by* MACIEJ SZCZEPANSKI.)

GIEREK: (*On monitor*) But strikes do not change anything for the better. Together we must find another way. We must do it for Poland's sake.

(*This is the end of* GIEREK's *speech. He pauses a moment and then relaxes as* SZCZEPANSKI *approaches him.*)

SZCZEPANSKI: Good . . . very good. Congratulations, Comrade First Secretary.

GIEREK: Thank you.

(GIEREK *is gathering up his papers. He stands up.*)

SZCZEPANSKI: By the way, what did you think of the bookcase?

(GIEREK *looks behind him as the bookcase, which is now seen to be a fake flat, is moved aside by two* PROP MEN.)

GIEREK: Nice. Very nice.


15. INT. SZCZEPANSKI'S OFFICE

SZCZEPANSKI *is mixing cocktails.*

SZCZEPANSKI: Edward, do things look bad?

GIEREK: For you, you mean?

SZCZEPANSKI: For me? Why for me? Try and come out this weekend, relax a little.

GIEREK: How many cars do you have, Maciej?

SZCZEPANSKI: Cars? I don't know. Who's counting?

GIEREK: Kania.

SZCZEPANSKI: Kania? And what does he make it?

GIEREK: Eighteen.

SZCZEPANSKI: Eighteen? Well, Comrade, you know . . . as Chairman of the State Committee for Radio and TV one has to get about.

GIEREK: How many houses? An aeroplane. A yacht. A health club staffed by young women with unusual qualifications. Yes, Comrade Kania has a file on you.

SZCZEPANSKI: That's his job.

GIEREK: Yes. He undoubtedly has a file on me too. How much was that little object you presented me with on my sixty-fifth birthday?

SZCZEPANSKI: Well, it was gold. All right – who built your country house? Twenty-three million zlotys. We serve the Party. The Party rewards us. What do you say, Edward?

GIEREK: I think I'll be busy this weekend.

39

## 16. INT. KURON'S FLAT. NIGHT

JACEK KURON *and* GEREMEK *are watching* GIEREK *on a television set.*

GIEREK: (*On television*) Attempts by irresponsible individuals and anarchic, anti-socialist groups to use stoppages for political ends and to incite tension are a dangerous aspect of recent events at plants on the Gdansk coast . . .

(GIEREK *continues but the* NARRATOR'*s voice takes over.*)

NARRATOR: (*Voice over*) Jacek Kuron, who now joins the story, had a strategy for freedom in a Communist state – pay lip service to Party rule while organizing into self-governing groups, like unions.

GEREMEK: I think he's talking about you, Jacek.

## 17. INT. GIEREK'S OFFICE. NIGHT

*We see what is apparently the studio bookcase but the middle of it is a concealed door which now opens.* GIEREK *comes through the bookcase to his desk and we see that behind him there is another office with a* SECRETARY *at a desk. The phone on* GIEREK'*s desk is ringing.* GIEREK *picks it up. He listens for a moment.*

GIEREK: Lock him up.

## 18. EXT. STREET. NIGHT

KURON *and* GEREMEK *are walking down the street.*

NARRATOR: (*Voice over*) Back in the sixties Kuron was a radical Marxist calling for a revolutionary workers' state. The Polish United Workers' Party did not appreciate him and put him in gaol.

(KURON, *in conversation, bursts out laughing.*)

KURON: (*Cheerfully*) Now I'm rehabilitated. But I'm still followed by the police.

(*The camera tracks with them and finds the* NARRATOR *in the foreground.*)

NARRATOR: (*To camera*) The Polish intellectuals played no part in the rebellion in 1970 which brought Edward Gierek to power. But in '76 when Gierek had to survive the first rebellion of his own, Kuron and others, shocked by the brutal police repression, formed the Workers' Defence Committee.

(*Tracking again with* KURON:)

KURON: (*To* GEREMEK) The Workers' Defence Committee was formed out of shame. When you get to Gdansk, tell them that this time we won't just leave them to it. This thing could be amazing. Workers' power, economic power, not a rebellion but a social force. No blood in the streets. That belongs to history.

GEREMEK: You think so?

KURON: Don't you?

GEREMEK: History is my subject.

(*They come to a corner and shake hands to separate.* GEREMEK *moves off. Two* POLICEMEN *approach* KURON *and arrest him, without drama, and walk him towards a nearby police car. The* NARRATOR *is in the street watching this.*)

NARRATOR: Kuron and fourteen others were arrested on August 20th. For Gierek the subversive influence of the intellectual mavericks was the single most important factor underlying the Polish crisis . . .

(*He is interrupted by the* WITNESS, *who is now drunk.*)

WITNESS: Horse manure.

(*The* NARRATOR *turns.*)

NARRATOR: What is?

WITNESS: Kuron and his friends have been overtaken by events and they're still trying to catch up.

NARRATOR: Then why arrest them?

WITNESS: Gierek has got to arrest *someone*. Every day Brezhnev wants to know what's being done. Every day the answer is – nothing! Worse than nothing – negotiations instead of breaking heads. So Gierek arrests a few intellectuals. The Russians understand that. They've read Marx. Gierek knows it's irrelevant.

NARRATOR: Why doesn't he arrest the strikers instead?

WITNESS: He can't afford to.

NARRATOR: You mean he's scared? Or broke?

WITNESS: Try the money.

(*Another camera angle. The* WITNESS *weaves his way down the street. The* NARRATOR *faces the camera.*)

NARRATOR: Meanwhile, the economic situation was the single most important factor underlying –

(*The* WITNESS *turns round and shouts to the* NARRATOR.)

WITNESS: That's the one!

(*The camera tracks along the street, following a long fence on which graffiti have been scrawled, crude pictures illustrating the* NARRATOR's *next speech.*)

NARRATOR: (*Voice over*) Edward Gierek came to power promising political and economic reforms. He intended to go down in history as the man who turned Poland into a modern industrial nation. And for a while it worked. Life became freer and richer. The relaxation lasted a couple of years. The money lasted longer, but it was all borrowed – two billion by the middle of the decade, from the West alone. The idea was that the money would be turned into tractors, colour TVs, Polish Fiats . . . and then back into money. But almost everything Polish, except what came out of the ground, had a Western component which had to be paid for in hard currency to keep the expensive new factories in production, and with the oil crisis in 1973 those prices went up so more had to be borrowed, until Poland's industry was working just to pay the interest on a debt which, by 1980, topped 20 billion dollars.

19. INT. BOARD ROOM (BANK). DAY

*Formal meeting room. There is a 'round table' of* BANKERS, FINANSKY *among them. The* NARRATOR's *speech overlaps into this scene.*

FINANSKY: When we met in April I proposed a loan of 500 million dollars which would enable us to refinance our accumulated debt. This agreement proposes only 325 millions. In addition you propose a rate of interest above the Eurodollar rate. This is disappointing, gentlemen. You are endangering our ability to repay. This is the truth.

GERMAN BANKER: Minister, we represent more than 400 banks from sixteen countries. To service your debt requires 95 per cent of your export revenue.

AMERICAN BANKER: American banks are badly exposed. 1.7 billion dollars. Just the commercial banks, quite apart from a billion dollars in credits from my Government.

FINANSKY: American banks are lending the same to Peru.

AMERICAN BANKER: Yes, and ten times as much to Brazil. But

these countries are members of the International Monetary Fund, so the money does not come without strings. We are in a position to insist on certain controls. In your case we have no control.

SWISS BANKER: Your exports are being hit now with these strikes . . .

FINANSKY: (*Sharply*) The strikes are in response to the price increases which we were left in no doubt would be welcome to *you* gentlemen when we began these present negotiations.

AMERICAN BANKER: (*To his neighbour*) Well, isn't that something? If Poland goes down the drain it'll be the fault of Chase Manhattan.


20. INT. EXECUTIVE WASHROOM. DAY

GIEREK *is using a wash-basin. When he looks into the mirror in front of him he sees two well-dressed, well-shaved, well-groomed members of the Politburo,* JAGIELSKI *and* BARCIKOWSKI. *They are standing respectfully behind him, for instruction.* GIEREK *busies himself with soap and water while he talks.*

GIEREK: (*To* JAGIELSKI) In the Lenin shipyard there is a strike committee representing 380 places of work.

(JAGIELSKI *raises his eyebrows in surprise.*)

Yes, we tried to split them with separate deals but they weren't having that. (*To* BARCIKOWSKI) There are 25,000 on strike in Szczecin now. You will find a strike committee waiting to negotiate.

JAGIELSKI: Kania says in Gdansk they have a list of sixteen demands.

GIEREK: Twenty-one. Well, when they add the moon it will be twenty-two.

BARCIKOWSKI: Is that what we promise them?

GIEREK: Just end the strike. (*To* JAGIELSKI) You did it with the railway workers in July. You can do it with the shipyard. (GIEREK *ducks down to wash his face.*)


21. INT. THE SAME

As GIEREK *straightens we see he is now dry, and tying up his tie. In the mirror he sees* JAGIELSKI *and* BARCIKOWSKI *returning now in very different shape, unshaven, looking as though they had slept in their clothes, exhausted.*

BARCIKOWSKI: In Szczecin they make thirty-six demands beginning with free independent parties.

GIEREK: You mean unions.

BARCIKOWSKI: No. Parties. Political parties.

GIEREK: This is becoming grotesque.

BARCIKOWSKI: I told them I had come to discuss workers' grievances, not an overthrow of the political system. They accepted my point.

GIEREK: Good.

BARCIKOWSKI: And they told me that the first grievance is that the official union does not represent the workers' interest. The demand for free unions is central, absolutely central. The workers' spokesman in Szczecin is a veteran of 1970 – Marian Jurczyk – a strong Catholic. He demands also that Sunday Mass is broadcast on state radio. He is tough, very quiet, hard. When I arrived he did not even return my greeting. He said – these are our demands. The atmosphere is sober, unrelenting. No journalists, no cameras.

JAGIELSKI: Gdansk is a circus. The negotiations are in a room with a glass wall. On the other side of the glass there are hundreds of people. No, not a circus, a zoo. Scores of photographers. And every word we speak is broadcast all over the shipyard. Walesa does most of their talking. He is friendly, no intellectual but sharp, and he has the workers behind him like a football hero.

BARCIKOWSKI: The situation is very strange – some of these are our own people, *Party members!* You understand me, Comrade First Secretary? The Party itself is unstable.

(GIEREK, BARCIKOWSKI, JAGIELSKI *leave the washroom. The* WITNESS *(in the role of washroom attendant) approaches the mirror to tidy up after* GIEREK.)

NARRATOR: (*Voice over*) Gierek's chief concern now was to maintain the Party line –

(*The* WITNESS, *busy cleaning the wash-basin, looks up into the mirror, interrupting the* NARRATOR's *speech with a shake of his head.*)

(*Correcting himself*) – was to survive.

(*The* WITNESS *nods approvingly.*)

44

### 22. INT. SZCZEPANSKI'S OFFICE. NIGHT

*There are sounds of a party going on next door.* SZCZEPANSKI, *drinking, is brooding alone, watching* GIEREK *mouthing silently on television. Using a remote control he switches on a video recorder and Gierek's image is replaced by a mildly pornographic film. Meanwhile the* NARRATOR *is heard.*

NARRATOR: (*Voice over*) A crisis meeting of the Central Committee made a dramatic show of cleaning out the stables. Four Politburo members were sacked including the Prime Minister and the official trades union chief. There was a simultaneous purge of Party men in high government posts, including the Chairman of the State Committee for Radio and Television. Gierek was spared, confessing to . . .
(SZCZEPANSKI *switches the television set back to* GIEREK.)

GIEREK: (*On television*) . . . errors, inconsistencies, delays and hesitations. We owe an apology to those comrades who pointed out irregularities, who tried to do something about them . . .
(*The office door opens, increasing the sound of the party music. A party guest, a* GIRL, *enters.*)

GIRL: Come on, Maciej – the party's started without you.

SZCZEPANSKI: No. It's over.


### 23. INT. TELEVISION STUDIO

*For the moment we don't know if we are in the television studio or Gierek's actual office.* GIEREK *sits at his desk, the bookcase behind him. He has evidently just finished addressing the camera. He looks shattered. Abruptly he moves his chair back. It hits the bookcase, which topples over.*


### 24. INT. GIEREK'S OFFICE. NIGHT

*Now* GIEREK *is at his 'real' desk with the 'real' bookcase behind him.* GIEREK, *evidently at the end of his tether, mutters . . .*

GIEREK: What will the Russians do?

NARRATOR: (*Voice over*) The single most important factor underlying Poland's independence was, needless to say –

WITNESS: (*Voice over*) The Church.
(*Behind* GIEREK *the bookcase door opens. The* SECRETARY *is*

45

*showing in* CARDINAL WYSZYNSKI.)

25. INT. CAFE. NIGHT

*The* NARRATOR *and the* WITNESS *are sitting at a café table.*

NARRATOR: (*To* WITNESS) The Church?

WITNESS: The Church. Lech Walesa wears the Black Madonna of Częstochowa on his coat. The King of Poland consecrated the nation to her as recently as 1656 and just the day before yesterday when for the whole of the nineteenth century there was no such place, the Poles called their country the Christ among nations, and in the Church they kept alive the promise of resurrection. As with the Tsars so with Stalin. The years of terror discredited the political guardians of the nation state, and so the moral leadership fell to the Church. For the last thirty-two years that has meant to Cardinal Wyszynski.

26. INT. GIEREK'S OFFICE. NIGHT

*We pick up the shot as* WYSZYNSKI *is being shown into the room.*

NARRATOR: (*Voice over*) Imprisoned and conciliated, from the first years of Stalinist terror to the last years of Gierek's ramshackle version of the consumer society, Cardinal Wyszynski had been the spiritual leader of a people who by the irony of history constituted the most vital Catholic nation in Europe.

(*Door shuts.*)

GIEREK: Father, there will be blood. They won't listen. They will lose everything. You must talk to them before it's too late.

WYSZYNSKI: The Politburo?

GIEREK: The workers! The strikers! They demand things which cannot be given.

WYSZYNSKI: They demand nothing which is not their right. It is you who must listen. Or there will be blood. You will lose everything.

GIEREK: No — no. The Russians will intervene if we don't go back. You must save us. Save the Church.

WYSZYNSKI: The Church needs to be defended sometimes but it does not need to be saved.

46

GIEREK: (*Weeping*) Then save Poland . . .
(WYSZYNSKI *gets up and leaves the room.*)

27. INT. ANTE-ROOM. CONTINUATION

KANIA *is waiting outside.*

KANIA: (*To* WYSZYNSKI) How is he?

WYSZYNSKI: Better than I have seen him for a long time.

KANIA: His nerve has gone.

WYSZYNSKI: If you like.

KANIA: Can you help?

WYSZYNSKI: The Church does not resist an appeal. I will preach
on Tuesday. It is the Feast of the Black Madonna of
Częstochowa. I will speak as I must for the rights of
workers.

KANIA: These strikes harm the nation. We can't fulfil every
demand at once.

WYSZYNSKI: I will speak the whole truth.

KANIA: How many will hear you?

WYSZYNSKI: My voice carries.

KANIA: With your permission I will assist it with television
cameras.

WYSZYNSKI: Not with my permission.

28. INT. PARTY HEADQUARTERS (POLITBURO). DAY

*The Politburo is meeting.* GIEREK *sits in his usual place.* BABIUCH
*and* SZYDLAK *have gone.* (*Two other Politburo members, anonymous
ones as far as we are concerned, have also been sacked, and there are
three new faces round the table.*)

KANIA: We are no longer talking about the Baltic ports. There
are strikes in Wroclaw, in Warsaw, in the steel works, in
the mines of Silesia.
(*The door opens as* KANIA *is speaking to admit a latecomer,*
STEFAN OLSZOWSKI. OLSZOWSKI *without ceremony responds to*
KANIA.)

OLSZOWSKI: What about the army?

KANIA: Welcome, Comrade Olszowski.

JARUZELSKI: Welcome back, Comrade Olszowski.
(*The* MEMBERS *get up generally and shake* OLSZOWSKI's *hand
and welcome him back.* OLSZOWSKI *sits down.*)

47

KANIA: Congratulations on your re-election. How was Berlin?

OLSZOWSKI: (*Sitting down*) The Germans think we're soft. If we don't act now, with troops if necessary, we deserve what we get.

(*He looks directly at* JARUZELSKI.)

JARUZELSKI: Yes. But not yet.

OLSZOWSKI: When?

JARUZELSKI: When there is no alternative.

OLSZOWSKI: When is that?

JARUZELSKI: I don't know. I'll tell you.

OLSZOWSKI: Next week? Next year?

JARUZELSKI: It depends on them.

OLSZOWSKI: *On them?*

JARUZELSKI: Oh yes. We must give them what they demand and then it depends on them. They will bring us to it, slowly or quickly, but we'll get there, you have my guarantee.

OLSZOWSKI: (*To* GIEREK) Comrade First Secretary . . .

GIEREK: (*To* JAGIELSKI) Comrade Jagielski . . . go back to Gdansk and sign.

## 29. EXT. GDANSK SHIPYARD. DAY

*There is a large crowd of noisy, celebrating* DOCK WORKERS *and one man elevated above them on the shoulders of his fellow workers* — WALESA.

NARRATOR: (*Voice over*) Jagielski and Lech Walesa signed the Gdansk Agreement on August 31st. The impossible had taken sixteen days. The inevitable was going to take sixteen months.

# Part Two: Solidarity

30. INT. PRISON. DAY

JACEK KURON *is released from a prison cell by two* GUARDS.

NARRATOR: (*Voice over*) The piece of paper signed in Gdansk guaranteed much more than an independent trade union. It spelled out the right to strike, freedom of expression, the broadcasting of Mass, economic reforms, medical, housing and welfare benefits, pensions and . . .

(*The* POLICEMAN *leads* KURON *along the catwalk*.)

. . . the freeing of political prisoners.

(KURON *and his* ESCORT *walk along a corridor lined with cells. From one of these a* PRISONER *shouts at him*.)

PRISONER: Hey, Kuron! – is it just the bloody intelligentsia who are being let out? I've redistributed more property than you'll ever see!

NARRATOR: (*Voice over*) Kuron went straight to Gdansk. For two decades the drama of his intellectual life had been the attempt to square the Communist circle inside the cornerstones of democratic socialism, and now the show had started without him.

31. EXT. STREET (GDANSK). DAY

WALESA *is coming down the street in a scrum of people, mostly* JOURNALISTS, *some with notebooks and some with tape recorders and microphones. Passers-by and general public are also drawn to the scrum which is quite a large crowd of people altogether, thirty or forty. It is a travelling press conference, with the questions distributed among the* JOURNALISTS, *sometimes shouted from the fringe of the scrum.*

QUESTION: Lech, what are you going to do next?

WALESA: Eat dinner.

QUESTION: What is your dream?

WALESA: For Poland to be Poland.

QUESTION: What does that take?

WALESA: To eat dinner. To speak what we think. To come and go as we please.

QUESTION: Are you a Marxist?

WALESA: How do I know? I never read a book.

QUESTION: What is your badge?

WALESA: (*Touching the badge on his lapel*) The Black Madonna of Częstochowa, the holiest shrine in Poland. Here I have a picture of her –

(*He has small photographs of the Madonna which he hands out as he walks.*)

QUESTION: What is your main task?

WALESA: To keep the movement together.

QUESTION: Why are you the leader?

WALESA: I'm the chairman. I'm not a dictator. Maybe a democratic dictator.

QUESTION: What do you want to be?

WALESA: When I was an electrician I wanted to be the best.

QUESTION: What is the first thing the union has to do?

WALESA: Survive.

QUESTION: Who is the greatest danger, Russia or the Party?

WALESA: Neither. Our greatest danger is ourselves. We must learn restraint and patience or we'll tear ourselves apart.

QUESTION: Do you want to overthrow the Party?

WALESA: No – I want the Party to be strong and to be just. A weak party would be disastrous. I would have to join it.

QUESTION: Isn't the union a challenge to the Party?

WALESA: The workers challenge themselves. They let themselves down.

QUESTION: Do you want to go to America?

WALESA: I want to go everywhere and with Mother Mary on my coat I will. But now I want to go home. As a husband and father I also want to be the best. Also as a lover. I have six children and my wife won't forgive me for getting mixed up in this. I will have to give her a seventh.

(*He is extricating himself from the crowd.*)

QUESTION: Lech – are you scared?

WALESA: I am scared of nothing and nobody, only of God.
(*He has arrived at the doorway to the block of flats where he lives. He disappears inside.*)


32. INT. FLATS. DAY

WALESA *comes up the staircase. On a landing there is a small* CHILD (*one of Walesa's children*).

WALESA: What have you been doing?

CHILD: Having my picture taken.

(WALESA *takes the* CHILD *by the hand and continues up the stairs and then enters his own flat.*)


33. INT. WALESA FLAT. DAY

*There are several* PHOTOGRAPHERS *in the flat taking photographs of the other* CHILDREN *and of* DANUTA (*Mrs Walesa*). *She gives him a rueful look. He smiles and shrugs.*

*The* PHOTOGRAPHERS *turn their attention to* WALESA. *He sees that the phone is off the hook. He replaces it.*

JOURNALIST: Here, Lech . . .

(*A* JOURNALIST *gives* WALESA *a carton of American* (*Marlboro*) *cigarettes.* WALESA *nods and smiles. The phone rings.*)


34. INT. BATHROOM (THE FLAT). DAY

WALESA *is in the bath, pouring water over his head.*

PHOTOGRAPHER: (*Off screen*) This way, Lech.

(*We see that there is a* PHOTOGRAPHER *in the bathroom with him. The* PHOTOGRAPHER *takes several photographs using a motordrive camera.*)

NARRATOR: (*Voice over*) Everyone knew that Lech was special. Pretty soon the outside world learned not to call him Walesser or Valesser but Vawensa.


35. INT. SOLIDARITY MEETING ROOM. DAY

*The meeting room is crowded.* SOLIDARITY MEMBERS *are meeting each other, shaking hands. The crowd includes Solidarity's* 'ADVISERS'. *There is a good deal of self-introduction going on as the* NARRATOR's *speech identifies several of the individuals we are going to be concerned with.*

NARRATOR: (*Voice over*) The names and faces multiply, and

there were many more than these. But it sorts itself out like this . . .

The intellectuals who formed themselves around the union as unofficial advisers included . . . Kuron . . . Geremek, the historian . . . Mazowiecki, a radical Catholic journalist . . . and Modzelewski, who had gone to gaol with Kuron in 1967 when the two of them, both radical Communists and lecturers at Warsaw University, had written an open letter attacking Party rule. Mazowiecki became Solidarity's press spokesman. Jurczyk, a storeman, led the strikers at Szczecin . . . Gwiazda was the man perhaps closest to Walesa. Allowing for simple demarcations, Gwiazda . . . and Rulewski, who led one of the regional branches of the union, were radicals who were to come into conflict with Walesa's more moderate line . . . Lis personified one of the paradoxes of the situation, for he was a member of the Communist Party . . . Bujak was the union's leader in Warsaw . . . and there were others like these whose names the outside world never did get right, because—

36. EXT. SHIPYARD. DAY

NARRATOR: (*Voice over*)—the personality cult grew—sensationally—around a 37-year-old electrician whose combative, streetwise style had marked him out long before he climbed over the steel fence of the Lenin shipyard and found himself famous.

(WALESA *has been walking through the shipyard, carrying a yard-high model of the 'Gdansk Memorial'. He is greeted on all sides by* WORKERS, *and greetings are shouted at him from distant perches on cranes and gantries.* WALESA *acknowledges the treatment like a star.*)

He liked the attention. In months to come he would be on scores of magazine covers and travel as far as Japan, meeting the great. It caused resentment inside Solidarity, but that was later.

37. INT. SOLIDARITY MEETING ROOM. CONTINUATION

WALESA, *carrying the model of the memorial, enters the room. He sees*

KURON *there and shouts towards him.*

WALESA: Jacek . . . they let you out . . . do you want to make a
speech?

KURON: It's your revolution. You tell us what you want us to do.
(*The meeting settles down around* WALESA. WALESA *puts the
model of the memorial on the table.*)

WALESA: We have to make an organization. Suddenly everyone
has a free union. All over the country they're saying, we'll
have the same as Gdansk, thank you very much. I don't
know. Maybe there should be no centralization; just separate
unions.

MAZOWIECKI: No. You have to be national, otherwise the Party
will pick you off piece by piece –

GEREMEK: – or break down into chaos trying to deal with you
separately. You have to have dialogue, not a general racket
going on. Stability. Discipline.

WALESA: So a national commission representing all the regions?

MAZOWIECKI: Right.

WALESA: Yes – yes – you're right – we have to act as one.

BUJAK: You mean if we want to strike in Warsaw we have to come
to Gdansk for permission?

WALESA: Yes – definitely –

GWIAZDA: What are we going to be? An alternative bureaucracy?
A Politburo?

WALESA: How we use our authority is up to us. If we are fair we
will use it fairly. For the good of all.

GWIAZDA: That's Party language, Lech.

WALESA: No, it's the language of democracy, stolen by the Party.
We're a workers' movement, not a mob. Local strikes must
have a majority at factory level first, and then they must be
ratified by a majority at the National Commission in Gdansk.

JURCZYK: What is this Gdansk – Gdansk – Gdansk? We had a
strike at Szczecin. *We* also had a member of the Politburo on
his knees. *We* also signed an agreement. We had everything
you had except foreign journalists, and you should have told
them to mind their own business like we did.

WALESA: I don't care if the National Commission meets in
Szczecin or Katowice. It can meet in different places. It can
meet in a hot air balloon for all I care.

MAZOWIECKI: Don't say that – the damn thing would never come down.

WALESA: All right. We don't even exist yet, legally. All we have is a name. (*To* KURON) We're taking the name of the strike bulletin we published in the yard.

(*He gives* KURON *a copy of the bulletin.* KURON *looks at it.*)

KURON: Solidarity.

WALESA: We'll have legal registration in a few weeks. The statutes are being drafted now by our legal experts. You see, intellectuals have their uses – though we had trouble with them at first. They kept putting the word socialist into the manifestos, and the workers kept taking it out.

KURON: Well, we didn't know you were thinking of changing the political system.

WALESA: We aren't. We don't want to govern. We don't want to be a threat.

GWIAZDA: What are you talking about? We *are* a threat. And we are dealing with gangsters.

WALESA: We're a union, that's all.

GWIAZDA: Do you believe that?

WALESA: If we don't believe it, how can *they*? Look, it's like this. The workers want bread. A decent wage. And a proper machinery to represent them, to take their side, and also a proper influence on the way things are managed at work. We're not political.

GWIAZDA: Most of our demands are political. What's the most important thing we've gained?

JURCZYK: The broadcasting of Mass.

GWIAZDA: Jesus God.

JURCZYK: Please don't blaspheme.

GWIAZDA: Abolition of censorship – the right to strike – free elections for the union – no more Party hacks holding down jobs they don't know how to do – *free trade unions are political*.

MAZOWIECKI: He's right.

GWIAZDA: We're going to have to fight just to keep what we've won – even to *get* what we've won. You'll see when they start breaking their promises.

WALESA: (*To* KURON) Is he right?

KURON: I said it was a revolution. The trick is to make it a self-limiting revolution. The Party must keep the leading role.

LIS: I'm still a Party member. Lenin said the unions were the connection between the Party and the workers.

KURON: And with a union controlled by the Party there's no problem. But an uncontrolled union reverses the current of power. The Party won't forgive. It will give up ground and take its time, but in the end they still have the police and the security forces. So go slowly. You can win little by little, but remember, if you lose you will lose overnight. (*Snaps his fingers.*) Like that.

(*Everyone is sobered by this. The camera looks from face to face.* WALESA *is looking at the model of the memorial.* KURON *approaches him.*)

WALESA: Look at this, Jacek. It's going to be forty metres high, outside the gate. We used to show up there every December. With stones in our suitcases. We'd make a little monument and the police would kick it over and take us away. They won't kick this over in a hurry.

KURON: I've always said that workers shouldn't elect leaders . . . it makes it too easy for the Party to identify the enemy.

WALESA: We'll have safety in numbers. Thousands and thousands are joining. Party members, too. They understand. We're not an opposition. We're reformers. The Party needs reforming more than anybody else. Don't worry. We'll have 10 million members.

(KURON *smiles at this.*)

I said we'd have a monument. Now I say we'll have 10 million members.


38. INT. PARLIAMENT. DAY

*The cut is to the members of the Politburo who appear to be sitting in the dock of a courtroom. There are twelve of them, including* GIEREK, JARUZELSKI, KANIA, FINANSKY, PINKOWSKI (*the Prime Minister*) *and* OLSZOWSKI. GIEREK *is absent. The 'dock' is actually the Politburo bench in parliament.*

SPEAKER ONE: What we have witnessed in Gdansk, Comrades, is an attack on the state organized by anarchists and anti-socialist groups –

(*This is greeted off screen by loud protests.*)

SPEAKER TWO: No, that's not true – these are genuine grievances – there is a failure in the Party, and it is at the top of the Party!

(*The applause for this covers the narration.*)

NARRATOR: (*Voice over*) This was parliament five days after the Gdansk signing. The usual ventriloquist act had fallen apart. The dummy had come to life.

SPEAKER THREE: We have become a rubber stamp for a Party leadership which has lost its way. We are a sham society built on propaganda which has become a joke. We have sham planning, sham achievements in industry and science, sham debates, sham elections, sham socialism, sham justice, sham morality, and finally sham contentment because no one can any longer tell the sham from the real.

(*More applause over which –*)

NARRATOR: (*Voice over*) The other odd thing was that the First Secretary, Edward Gierek, was missing, and there was no news of him.


39. INT. HOSPITAL VESTIBULE. EVENING

KANIA, *carrying a large bunch of flowers, crosses.*


40. INT. PRIVATE WARD. EVENING

*The room is so full of people that at first one doesn't realize that* GIEREK *is in the hospital bed, apparently unconscious. The people in the room are the Politburo, who are animatedly discussing the situation in small groups . . . eating the grapes, drinking the barley water, examining the patient's chart.* OLSZOWSKI *is wearing head-phones, the hospital radio, and manipulating the wall-switch which changes the channels: the switch is heavily labelled,* Light music, Warsaw, Moscow, East Berlin, Prague.

KANIA *enters.*

JARUZELSKI: (*To* KANIA) Gierek's had a heart attack. The Central Committee is meeting tonight. We'll have a new first secretary by the morning.

KANIA: Does Stefan have hopes?

OLSZOWSKI: Quiet. I can't hear a thing.

NARRATOR: (*Voice over*) Stefan Olszowski had been in the Politburo before until a disagreement over Gierek's economic policy shunted him into the Ambassador's job in East Berlin. Now the Central Committee had brought him back. There was a hard line in the Party and Olszowski spoke for it.

OLSZOWSKI: Moscow says there are no inherent defects in the socialist system, it's in the weakness of the leadership. (*Turns the dial from* Moscow *to* East Berlin.) And as for the Germans . . .
(*He reels back as the Germans nearly blow his ear out.*)

41. INT. CAFE. NIGHT

*The* NARRATOR *and the* WITNESS *are at a table playing chess. It seems to be the* WITNESS's *move. He is frowning at the board.*

NARRATOR: (*To camera*) But the Central Committee did not advance Stefan Olszowski. It was not the moment to attack on the left.

WITNESS: Why is it always *chess*?

NARRATOR: Ugh, well, you know, it symbolizes . . .

WITNESS: These ones with horse's heads, are they the ones which can jump over things?

NARRATOR: You're ruining it.

WITNESS: Sorry.

NARRATOR: (*To camera*) The mood was for reform, renewal, nothing too liberal, but no conservative backlash. A middle-of-the-road *apparatchik* with a tough background in security but with nothing of the zealot about him would do. Kania had the job by 2 a.m.

42. INT. KREMLIN. DAY

BREZHNEV *and a* SECRETARY, *in an office.* BREZHNEV *is standing on a chair being measured by a* TAILOR.

BREZHNEV: (*dictating*) Dear Kania – get things back to normal or we'll be down on you like a ton of bricks. Read that back.

SECRETARY: Dear Comrade Kania, the working people of the Soviet Union know you as a staunch champion of the people's true interests, the ideals of Communism, the strengthening of the leading role of the Party, and the consolidation of socialism in the Polish People's Republic. (*It goes on like that but we fade him out . . .*)

NARRATOR: (*Voice over*) But Kania, in his first public statement, pledged himself to the spirit of Gdansk.

### 43. INT. KANIA'S OFFICE. DAY

KANIA *is behind his desk.*

KANIA: (*To camera*) The Party will reform itself, workers will work, the citizens will have more freedom, the newspapers will report the facts, radio will broadcast Mass, the hacks will be sacked, corruption will be stamped out, and Poland will be in charge of her own destiny throughout. It's all going to be all right.

### 44. INT. CAFE. DAY

*The* NARRATOR *and the* WITNESS *are now playing cards.*

WITNESS: Twist.

(*The* NARRATOR *deals him a card.*)

NARRATOR: (*To camera*) But it was a bluff and Kania knew it.

WITNESS: Bust.

### 45. INT. KANIA'S OFFICE. DAY

KANIA *is behind his desk as before.*

KANIA: The Soviet Union supplies us with all our crude oil, potash, and iron ore, and 80 per cent of our natural gas and our timber. The August strikes have cost us zillions of zlotys and they aren't finished. All over the place workers have caught Gdansk disease. And all over the place the fat cats of the Party apparatus and the old union are digging in against what they call an anti-socialist sell out. It's not going to be a picnic.

### 46. EXT. STEELWORKS. GDANSK. DAY

*Gate with flowers in foreground.*

*Camera drops to take in steelworks as gates are shut.*

NARRATOR: (*Voice over*) The wheel of reform was moving so slowly that to give it a shove the union announced a token one-hour strike for October 3rd. With a week to go, the Solidarity leadership came to Warsaw to apply for legal registration.

(*Hooters go off.*)

47. INT. COURTROOM. DAY

WALESA *is alone in the room. A door opens and* KANIA *enters.*

KANIA: Comrade Walesa . . .

(*They shake hands.*)

WALESA: Congratulations, Comrade First Secretary, on your elevation.

KANIA: Likewise. Please sit down, Comrade. Comrade Walesa, when I was elected First Secretary I told the Central Committee that I intended to use the collective wisdom of the people. A strike is not the act of wisdom.

WALESA: A stoppage, for one hour.

KANIA: But a million people, even for one hour, is a provocative symbol to our allies.

WALESA: It's going to be 3 million, Comrade First Secretary.

KANIA: I'm trying to help you but I have suspicious and angry people behind me.

WALESA: That's my position also.

(KANIA *thumps the table angrily.*)

KANIA: The proletariat cannot dictate to the Party what —

(*He collects himself. People are filing into the room. The two men begin whispering.*)

In the dictatorship of the proletariat, the Party must have the leading role.

WALESA: We accept that.

KANIA: But you haven't said so in the legal statutes which have been deposited with the Warsaw Provincial Court.

WALESA: We haven't said so because we are not a political organization. The leading role of the Party is nothing to do with us.

KANIA: The leading role of the Party is to do with everybody!

WALESA: To acknowledge it in the statutes *would* be a political act.

KANIA: To *refuse* to acknowledge it is a political act.

(*Now we see that the room is full of people.*)

WALESA: The independence of the free trade union Solidarity is not negotiable. We are waiting for the decision of the Court. Then we will know if this game is honest.

(*Close up on a* JUDGE.)

JUDGE: The registration of the independent trade union
Solidarity is allowed.

(*On the reverse shot* WALESA *smiles briefly at* GWIAZDA *who,
however, holds up his hand as if to say, 'Not so fast.'*)

But, the statutes of the union are modified to include the
acknowledgement of the leading role of the—

WALESA: The Court has no power to alter the statutes!

GWIAZDA: (*Furiously to* WALESA) Now will you believe me! We're
dealing with gangsters!


48. EXT. BALCONY. DAY

*We see a line-up of the* PARTY BOSSES, *just heads and shoulders
above the parapet. They are dressed like gangsters. They look out
front, possibly reviewing a parade, and talk among themselves out of
the sides of their mouths.*

KANIA: The Walesa mob is calling a general strike.

OLSZOWSKI: Rub them out.

KANIA: There's 3 million of them!

GANG MEMBER: Four million, boss.

KANIA: Shut up!

JARUZELSKI: (*To* KANIA) It was the wrong time to pull a stunt
like that.


49. EXT. STREET. DAY

NARRATOR *and* WITNESS *appear to be among the crowd looking up at
the Politburo's balcony.*

WITNESS: What's all this gangster stuff?

NARRATOR: It's a metaphor.

WITNESS: Wrong. You people—

NARRATOR: All right.


50. EXT. BALCONY. DAY. CONTINUATION

*Now the people on the balcony are no longer dressed as gangsters.
They speak normally too.*

JARUZELSKI: It was the wrong time for a confrontation.

KANIA: You haven't had Comrade Brezhnev shouting down the
telephone—

JARUZELSKI: Comrade Brezhnev only demands stability. Throw

the dogs a few bones. Leave the statutes of the union as
they are, and put whatever you want into an appendix.
Walesa will help us if we help him. And when the time
comes . . .


51. INT. SOLIDARITY MEETING ROOM. DAY

WALESA, FAMILY *and* OTHERS *are kneeling. A* PRIEST *is holding
Mass.*

NARRATOR: (*Voice over*) And so the deal was made. Solidarity
was legal. And Mass was on the radio. The regime lost face
but stood to gain a period of calm – so long as the moderate
men on either side were in control.


52. INT. WARSAW SOLIDARITY OFFICE. NIGHT

*A Solidarity poster is on the office window. Close up of Solidarity
poster. A group of* POLICEMEN *enter the office and immediately begin
ransacking it. The only occupant is* BUJAK. BUJAK *stands up.*

NARRATOR: (*Voice over*) The calm lasted nine days.

BUJAK: What the hell is going on?

(*The* OFFICER IN CHARGE *hands him the warrant. The other*
OFFICERS *are emptying filing cabinet drawers on to the floor.*)


53. INT. KANIA'S BEDROOM. NIGHT

*Telephone rings. Light goes on.* KANIA *picks up receiver.*

KANIA: (*Angrily*) On whose orders?


54. INT. WALESA'S FLAT. NIGHT

*The phone is ringing.* WALESA, *in night clothes, finally answers it.*

WALESA: (*Into phone*) Yes – ?

(*In the near dark he listens and feels for the light switch. He
puts the light on.*)

Jesus and Mary . . .


55. INT. SOLIDARITY MEETING ROOM. GDANSK. DAY

*A meeting of the Praesidium with* WALESA *in the chair. There are
about a dozen others including a young woman* (ALINA PIENKOWSKA)
*and* BOGDAN LIS *and* ANDRZEJ GWIAZDA. BUJAK, *talking to them, is
the only one standing up.*

BUJAK: They broke into the Solidarity office in Warsaw and

found what they say is a secret document. They have arrested our printer and also a clerk in the Prosecutor's office. They claim he leaked the document to us. Warsaw Solidarity has called a strike of the entire region, if both men are not released.

WALESA: Excuse me. A strike is not called by a regional office, only by the National Commission of the Union.

BUJAK: Then you'd better call it. Work has already stopped at Ursus Tractors. What's more we are demanding as a condition of calling off the strike an investigation into the methods of the Prosecutor's office and of the security police. We're demanding cuts in the police budget and also the punishment of those who committed the police brutalities in '70 and '76.

(WALESA *looks despairing.*)

WALESA: For two arrested men? And what do we hit them with when the stakes get higher?


56. INT. KANIA'S OFFICE. DAY

KANIA *has the* PUBLIC PROSECUTOR *standing across the desk.*

KANIA: Comrade Prosecutor – are we to have a confrontation with a million workers over a miserable document?

PROSECUTOR: It is a classified document – a secret circular prepared by myself, on the organization of the anti-socialist groups. Furthermore, it is a stolen document. We have a good case for prosecution.

KANIA: (*Angrily*) The document contains nothing of importance. I have said on behalf of the Party, in public, that we offer Solidarity coexistence. These arrests merely make me look like a liar.


57. INT. SOLIDARITY MEETING ROOM. GDANSK. DAY

WALESA *and the Praesidium (same people as scene 55).*

WALESA: (*Strongly*) These demands against the security police – they can't be made in the name of the union. We are a non-political organization. It was a pledge. Do you want to ruin everything?

58. EXT. STEELWORKS. DAY

*It is snowing. A high shot shows us the works at a standstill. Groups of* STEEL WORKERS *stand around. A small group is waiting for* WALESA, BUJAK *and* KURON *who are walking purposefully towards the waiting delegation of* WORKERS.

*When the two small groups arrive face to face we go into a closer shot.*

BUJAK: Where can we talk?


59. EXT. STEELWORKS. DAY

BUJAK, KURON *and* WALESA *are huddled under the steps with the small group of* STEEL WORKERS, *one of whom acts as a spokesman. Snow continues to fall.*

BUJAK: It is very simple. We demanded the release of the two men. The Government has delivered them. We have to deliver the end of the strike.

STEEL WORKER: Our demands have not been satisfied.

WALESA: Your demands did not have the sanction of Gdansk.

STEEL WORKER: We are not in Gdansk. We are in Warsaw. Furthermore, our region is much bigger than the Gdansk region.

KURON: My friend, there is another reality beyond the immediate issue.

STEEL WORKER: Who is he?

KURON: I am Jacek Kuron.

STEEL WORKER: You're not a worker.

KURON: This is not an argument between you and the police. It is an argument between millions of Poles and the regime.

STEEL WORKER: No, it is between us and the police. In '76 when the Government raised prices we went on strike and we won. They caved in. Afterwards the police made us run the gauntlet of truncheons. We were beaten unconscious, they smashed our bones. Who was ever punished for those crimes?

KURON: (*Helplessly*) Lech?

WALESA: What can I say?

BUJAK: You don't have to tell these men about the police. They have been in cells and in gaol. The Government has agreed to talk about the responsibility of the police.

63

STEEL WORKER: In private they will say anything.

BUJAK: The talks on police were announced on television tonight.

STEEL WORKER: Talks is not what we asked for. They guarantee nothing.

WALESA: (*Rather dramatically*) I am your guarantee! (*Self-consciously he amends this.*) We are your guarantee.


60. INT. FIRST SECRETARY'S OFFICE (KANIA). MORNING

KANIA *is being shaved, by, as it turns out, the* WITNESS.

KANIA: There are people who think that the Party boss can run the operation like a Chicago gangster. They should try sitting in this chair. I've got a Party which is losing members in droves, and half of those who remain have joined a free trade union with 5 million members–

WITNESS: (*Discreetly correcting*) Seven million.

KANIA: (*Taking the correction without comment*) Seven million. With the right to strike for more money which I haven't got because industrial production is down 12 per cent owing to the strikes, so I have to go cap in hand to the Soviets who are giving us 690 million dollars in credits to keep Poland Communist. And to the United States who are giving us 550 million dollars for the same reason. I've got a rank and file which wants to know when I'm going to reform the middle apparatus, and I've got a middle apparatus which wants to know when I'm going to stop the rot in the rank and file, and a leadership which is waiting to see which way the cat will jump. I've got a Catholic Church which doesn't want me to provoke the Russians, and a Communist Party two-thirds of whom believe in God. And to top it all off I've got a police force which can't break the habit, and a Public Prosecutor with the political nous of a bull in a china shop. As First Secretary of the Polish United Workers' Party, Al Capone wouldn't have lasted out the week.

(*The* INTERCOM *on the desk announces* . . .)

INTERCOM: His Excellency the Soviet Ambassador is here.

## 61. INT. KANIA'S OFFICE. ANOTHER SECTION. DAY

KANIA *leads the* AMBASSADOR *into the room, shows him to a chair. They sit.*

KANIA: Good morning, Ambassador.

AMBASSADOR: Good morning, Comrade. You're looking tired.

KANIA: How can I help you, Ambassador?

AMBASSADOR: Comrade Brezhnev wishes to inform you that a meeting of the leaders of the Warsaw Pact is to take place in Moscow in eight days' time. Comrade Brezhnev asks me to convey his fraternal greetings and looks forward to seeing you on December 5th.

KANIA: (*Examining his diary*) I'll have to cancel a lunch. I accept with pleasure, of course. I ask you to return my greetings when you have an opportunity.

AMBASSADOR: I have many opportunities, Comrade First Secretary. Comrade Brezhnev is taking a very close interest in events here.

KANIA: Naturally. We are grateful for his interest.

AMBASSADOR: The situation is interesting. The Warsaw strike. The general strike which is due to begin in four hours . . .

KANIA: There are no Warsaw strikes this morning. There will be no general strike either.

AMBASSADOR: That is very good news. It is very important to us that the Party should not show weakness.

KANIA: Quite so.

AMBASSADOR: And your two prisoners?

KANIA: Prisoners?

AMBASSADOR: The saboteurs arrested a week ago.

KANIA: You have been misinformed, Ambassador. Two men were detained on suspicion but the suspicions proved unfounded. The men were released very early this morning.

AMBASSADOR: I see.

KANIA: It is delightful to have seen you again.

AMBASSADOR: You won't forget? Moscow, December 5th.

(*The* AMBASSADOR *stands up and leaves the room.*)


## 62. INT. KREMLIN. DAY

*This is the meeting of the Warsaw Pact leaders.* BREZHNEV *is chairman. The Polish group consists of* KANIA, PINKOWSKI (*the last-seen prime minister*), BARCIKOWSKI *and* OLSZOWSKI *and* JARUZELSKI. *There is a little Polish flag on the table in front of them. At intervals around the large table there are the flags of Hungary, East Germany, Poland, Romania and Czechoslovakia. The only person standing is one of the Germans who is halfway through a tirade, backed up by a pile of documents, including a sheaf of* Solidarity *magazines. He is referring to these one by one.*

GERMAN MINISTER: Item – a blatant attack on the person of the Regional Chairman of the Party. Item – a blatant attack on the office of the Public Prosecutor. Item – a blatant attack on the principle of peasant collectives. And so it goes on. These publications, openly printed and distributed by Solidarity, are an attack on socialism, an attack on everyone here, and I tell you this, Comrades, if the day comes when we in the German Democratic Republic allow the publication of filth like this, then you are free to assume that we objectively agree with it.

(*He sits down. Pause.* BREZHNEV *speaks without standing up, in a fairly friendly manner, looking straight across at the Polish leaders.*)

BREZHNEV: You know, we had our very own Soviet free trade union. I forget his name. He is in a lunatic asylum now, poor fellow . . . You see, a Communist Party which cannot defend itself is no damn use, that is the problem. If it cannot defend itself, it must be defended.

### 63. EXT. BUNKER. DAY

*All we see is a group of perhaps half a dozen very high-ranking* MILITARY OFFICERS *dressed in cold-weather greatcoats, standing at a vantage point, their attention on events in the distance, events characterized by the sounds of military vehicles and high explosives. It is a relaxed group. One or two of them may be smoking. Each of them has a pair of binoculars which he uses occasionally. The uniforms belong to the armies of the Warsaw Pact countries. We are concerned with* GENERAL JARUZELSKI *and* MARSHAL KULIKOV *who are standing next to each other. They are cold. They raise their binoculars.*

NARRATOR: (*Voice over*) During these December days reservists were called up in the Baltic Soviet Republics. Soviet troops camped under canvas on the Polish border, and Soviet warships were visible from the coast. The United States Intelligence announced that Russian invasion plans were complete.

(KULIKOV *lowers his binoculars.*)

KULIKOV: Well, I don't know what all this is doing to the Poles but it's scaring the hell out of the Americans.

JARUZELSKI: We can deal with our own problems, Marshal.

KULIKOV: We all hope so, Wojciech.


64. EXT. THE GDANSK MEMORIAL INAUGURATION. NIGHT

*A crowd of people holding candles. It is snowing. There is the sound of the* 'Lacrimosa' *Krzysztof Penderecki's Chorale.*
*The floodlights illuminate the Solidarity banners.*
*We see* WALESA *dressed up for the winter cold. He wears a brown anorak. Around him, casually but warmly dressed are other* WORKERS *and* LEADERS *of Solidarity. There are also the men of Warsaw in heavy overcoats. There is a* GENERAL *in uniform and an* ADMIRAL *in uniform. There are* PRIESTS.

NARRATOR: (*Voice over*) On December 16th, the rulers and the ruled came together to inaugurate the Gdansk Memorial to the dead of 1970. The Solidarity banners were consecrated by an Archbishop. There was an army general, an admiral, a deputy member of the Politburo, a government minister and the Head of State, the ageing Professor Jablonski. There were diplomats of many foreign countries. There were 150,000 people gathered outside the gates of the Lenin shipyard. Lech Walesa, unknown six months before, now leader of a union of 10 million workers, lit the flame. It was the first time in a Communist country that a government had erected a memorial to workers who had rebelled against the state. The First Secretary of the Polish United Workers' Party and the Soviet Ambassador did not attend.

# Part Three: Congress

### 65. INT. CONFESSIONAL. DAY

WALESA *with his ear pressed to the grille is listening intently and rapidly making notes in a notebook.*

NARRATOR: (*Voice over*) In the middle of January Lech Walesa went to Rome . . . and, according to Prague Radio, got his instructions straight from the Pope.

(*Caption*: Courtesy of Prague Radio)

WALESA: (*Muttering*) Yes, Father, attack the principles of socialist construction, very well, Father . . .

### 66. INT. SOLIDARITY MEETING ROOM. GDANSK. DAY

*A large, disorganized, rowdy meeting of Solidarity people. They are members of the National Commission and we know a few of them.*

NARRATOR: (*Voice over*) Solidarity was in fact in endless dispute with the Government, which seemed unable or unwilling to concede what had been agreed in Gdansk. The Government had back-tracked on the five-day week, access to the media, censorship, and the right of private farmers to set up a Rural Solidarity of their own. There were strikes and sit-ins all over the country. The National Commission tried to tidy all this up by calling for a one-hour general strike . . .

(*The meeting has suddenly pulled itself together, the background noise stilled as everybody there raises one arm in the air.*)

. . . while ordering an end to local strikes. But the second part of that had no effect . . .

(*The meeting once more disintegrates into dispute and noise.*)

The country seemed bemused and helpless in the face of all these demands. As always, there was a Polish joke for the occasion.

(*Caption*: Polish Joke)

(*The meeting is suddenly stilled as a* WORKER *shouts.*)

WORKER: I move that from now on we only work on Tuesdays!
(*The meeting agrees by acclamation. However, the* WITNESS, *who is present, raises his hand and the meeting goes quiet again to listen to him.*)

WITNESS: Do you mean every Tuesday?

## 67. INT. OFFICE (PRIME MINISTER). DAY

WALESA *and* PRIME MINISTER PINKOWSKI *are putting their signatures to a document.*

NARRATOR: (*Voice over*) Walesa went into a twelve-hour meeting with the Prime Minister who at this time and for several days to come was called Mr Pinkowski. They reached an agreement which pleased neither side. On February 9th, Pinkowski was replaced. In Poland such a change was normally cosmetic, but this time it looked different.

## 68. EXT. STREET. DAY

*An official car draws up and a fawning* FUNCTIONARY *comes up to open the rear door, out of which comes* PRIME MINISTER GENERAL JARUZELSKI.

NARRATOR: (*Voice over*) The new Prime Minister liked to make unannounced visits . . .

## 69. INT. FOOD SHOP. DAY

NARRATOR: (*Voice over*) . . . sometimes to shops.
(*There is busy activity in the shop. Groceries of all kinds are being hastily unpacked from boxes and placed on empty shelves. When the shelves look fairly full, the* PRIME MINISTER *and his* ENTOURAGE *are seen to enter the shop. There is much handshaking and smiling as the* GENERAL *passes through.*

JARUZELSKI: And how is the food distribution?

PARTY OFFICIAL: It is working very well, Comrade.

JARUZELSKI: Good, good.
(*He passes rapidly through. As soon as he has gone all the groceries are quickly removed and repacked.*)

NARRATOR: (*Voice over*) Jaruzelski began by asking for a three months' suspension of strike action – for, as he put it, ninety peaceful days. He got thirty-eight.

### 70. EXT. STREET. NIGHT

*The cut is to a fight. Smoke bombs. Crowds scatter.* RULEWSKI *and other men are being beaten up by a group of plain-clothes* SECURITY POLICE.

### 71. INT. HOSPITAL VESTIBULE. NIGHT

*A group is walking purposefully along the corridor towards us.*
WALESA *is in the lead. A* PRIEST *is behind him.*

NARRATOR: (*Voice over*) The trouble happened in Bydgoszcz where the farmers, with the support of the local Solidarity leader, Jan Rulewski, staged a peaceful protest against the authorities' refusal to allow an independent farmers' union. The uniformed militia were called but there was no violence until the plain-clothes state security police moved in. Rulewski was badly beaten up.

PRIEST: Wisdom. Not vengeance. Wisdom.

### 72. INT. HOSPITAL WARD. NIGHT

*The injured* RULEWSKI *is in bed.* WALESA *and the* PRIEST *enter the ward and come to the bed.*

RULEWSKI: Yes – I heard you had a priest now.

WALESA: Jan. How are you feeling?

RULEWSKI: No – you talk.

WALESA: A warning strike within the week. A general strike after that if we don't get satisfaction.

RULEWSKI: Somebody ordered it. This was an attack on Solidarity by the Government.

WALESA: No. It was an attack on the Government's agreement with Solidarity. That's the best way to play it. We'll announce a strike in support of the Government of General Jaruzelski.

### 73. INT. OFFICE. NIGHT

JARUZELSKI *holding a telephone.*

JARUZELSKI: Tell him not to do us any favours.

### 74. INT. PARTY HEADQUARTERS (VESTIBULE). NIGHT

MIECZYSLAW RAKOWSKI *is holding a telephone to his ear, listening.*

NARRATOR: (*Voice over*) Jaruzelski's first appointment was to make Mieczyslaw Rakowski Deputy Prime Minister with special responsibility for the unions. From now on, Rakowski, the editor of an influential political weekly, was going to do most of the talking to Solidarity.

(RAKOWSKI *has meanwhile put the phone down and approached* WALESA *who we now see is standing in the lobby*.)

RAKOWSKI: While we're standing here the armies of the Warsaw Pact are conducting exercises on Polish soil. Your warning strike was the greatest disruption of work in the history of this country.

(WALESA *looks surprised*.)

I mean in the history of the Polish People's Republic. If the general strike goes ahead we could end up with Soviet tanks lined up in the square outside.

WALESA: You've played the Russian card too many times. Blood has been spilled. Twenty-seven citizens of the Polish People's Republic who were not breaking any law have been injured in an assault by the state police in the city of Bydgoszcz. Three of them are in hospital. Does this have your approval?

RAKOWSKI: There will be an investigation, of course.

WALESA: Another card.

RAKOWSKI: We'll punish those responsible for the assault. You may have my guarantee. But the strike must be called off.

WALESA: It's not my decision. But your offer is not enough.

RAKOWSKI: All right, we also guarantee that the question of the farmers' union will be examined by a parliamentary commission. And you know what that means with this parliament. It'll only be a matter of time. But we can't move faster than the Party lets us. You understand. The Party must have the leading role. That is Communism.

WALESA: And independent unions, is that Communism?

RAKOWSKI: Don't underestimate Polish Communism. We've got less than twenty-four hours before the strike goes ahead and all this is put at risk. What are you going to do?

75. INT. SOLIDARITY MEETING ROOM (GDANSK). DAY
WALESA *is there with* GWIAZDA *and* MODZELEWSKI. GWIAZDA *is angry*.

GWIAZDA: No.

WALESA: We've got most of what we wanted.

GWIAZDA: It's not up to us. The National Commission decided on the strike. If it's going to be called off, the National Commission has to meet to vote on it.

WALESA: (*Desperately*) There isn't time for that. We have to make it an executive decision.

MODZELEWSKI: You mean *your* decision. This whole business has been about as democratic as a Pharaoh's court. You're taking too much upon yourself, Lech.

WALESA: Nobody wants this strike. Do you want it?

MODZELEWSKI: I don't want the strike. I don't want any part of this decision. We went to a lot of trouble to make a democratic union. This is just getting to be Walesa's circus. I'm going back to Wroclaw to teach my students about democracy — you can get yourself another press officer.

WALESA: You're making a dogma out of procedure. Right and wrong is more important. A strike now would be wrong. And there isn't time. I'm putting this to the vote of the Praesidium. Let it be on my head. When the National Commission has time to meet, they can have it on a platter.

MODZELEWSKI: Right. I resign. (*To* GWIAZDA) How about you?

WALESA: (*To* GWIAZDA) You can only resign once, Andrzej.

(MODZELEWSKI *starts to pick up his briefcase to leave.*)

GWIAZDA: They've split us.


76. INT. POLITBURO. DAY

*Everybody is there and the mood is buoyant.*

RAKOWSKI: (*Triumphantly*) We've split them!

(RAKOWSKI *is being slapped on the back by* JARUZELSKI . . .)

KANIA: That's it! Get them at each others' throats!

(*But this picture freezes and tears itself in half like a piece of paper with the sound of tearing paper.*)


77. INT. CAFE. DAY

*The* NARRATOR *is scribbling at a table. He stops and crumples up the paper and throws it away. He is being watched by the* WITNESS.

WITNESS: Try the other one.

78. INT. POLITBURO. DAY

*As before.*

RAKOWSKI: (*Gloomily*) We've split them!

KANIA: (*Gloomily*) How can we control them if they're at each
others' throats all the time?
(*The picture freezes and tears itself in half like paper with the
sound of tearing paper.*)


79. INT. CAFE. DAY

NARRATOR *and* WITNESS.

NARRATOR: I don't understand who's winning.

WITNESS: Or who's being split.

NARRATOR: (*Interested*) Is that it?

WITNESS: These people aren't smart. They're Party bosses.


80. INT. POLITBURO. DAY

*As before.*

KANIA: They've split us.

WITNESS: (*Voice over*) That's the one.

KANIA: In Torun there's a big Party meeting which we haven't
sanctioned which wants to speed up reform. In Katowice
there's another meeting which thinks Stalin is alive and well
and is practically begging the Soviets to come in and save
Communism. I've got hundreds of complaints from the
rank and file. People want to know why we haven't
punished the police who did the beating up. They want to
know why we haven't expelled more Party members for
bribery and theft, although we've expelled thousands. They
demand an emergency Party Congress and I can't stop it.
They will elect to the Congress hundreds of people we can't
rely on. In the grass roots of the Party there are meetings
between workers in different factories, different cities.
Lenin called it the sin of horizontalism. He organized the
Party on vertical lines, control from top to bottom. This is
why. I'm getting demands for secret voting for the Party
Congress, unlimited candidates, limited terms of office,
accountability to the base instead of to the leadership. How
long do you think we'd last if that happened? How long
would Comrade Brezhnev and his colleagues last if it started

73

to spread?

### 81. INT. KREMLIN. DAY

BREZHNEV *is dictating a letter. There is a* SECRETARY *taking it down.*

BREZHNEV: To the Central Committee of the Polish United
Workers' Party from the Central Committee of the
Communist Party of the Soviet Union. Dear lads. Let me
spell it out for you. You were elected by the last Party
Congress under Gierek, and quite obviously you're going to
be out on your neck when the next Party Congress meets
four weeks from now, so this is your last chance. When
Kania and Jaruzelski were here in December they kept
agreeing with me but ever since then they've let the Party
drift into open democracy, make that bourgeois democracy,
and look what happened to the Czechs just before *they* had
their emergency Congress in '68 – say no more.

### 82. INT. POLITBURO. DAY

OLSZOWSKI *is reading* BREZHNEV'*s letter to the chastened Politburo.*

OLSZOWSKI: This letter is an invitation to the Central Committee
to change the leadership. Brezhnev has lost faith in the
Polish Party. And who can blame him when even Soviet
war memorials in Warsaw are being defaced?

### 83. EXT. SOVIET WAR MEMORIAL. NIGHT

*The memorial has been daubed with white paint. Sitting on top of
the memorial busy with scrubbing brush and bucket of water, is*
WALESA. *Standing on the plinth, watching him, is* KURON.

WALESA: The memorials are being defaced by *provocateurs*. I've
offered to scrub them with my own hands, on TV if they
like. As a union we take no position on Russia.

KURON: You take every position including that one up there.
You started something which you can't stop. You want a
self-limiting revolution but it's like trying to limit influenza.

WALESA: Yes, it's those bloody workers. You give us freedom of
choice, and we choose freedom. What I want to know is,
how did *you* get to be called the intellectuals?

74

84. INT. BREZHNEV'S OFFICE (KREMLIN). DAY

BREZHNEV *is having a medical examination. He is stripped to the waist and is attended by a* DOCTOR.

BREZHNEV'S SECRETARY *is standing to one side holding a file.*

BREZHNEV: What's the latest?

DOCTOR: No change.

BREZHNEV: I mean him.

(*The* SECRETARY *steps forward.*)

SECRETARY: Which first, sir?

BREZHNEV: Afghanistan.

(*The* SECRETARY *shuffles his files.*)

No, Poland. The Central Committee. Reaction to my letter.

SECRETARY: A strong attack on Kania's leadership in the Central Committee, and calls for his resignation.

BREZHNEV: (*Pleased*) And they think I'm losing my touch.

SECRETARY: However . . .

BREZHNEV: However what?

SECRETARY: A counter-attack arguing that if the hard-liners take over, the country will be polarized, with civil disobedience and strikes, and if we invade, Soviet Communism will be finished in Poland and *détente* with the Americans will be dead.

BREZHNEV: (*As the* DOCTOR *takes his blood pressure*) *Now* he takes my blood pressure.

SECRETARY: The entire Politburo offered themselves for a vote of confidence. The Central Committee declined the offer and proposed no changes in the leadership.

BREZHNEV: I see. And the Emergency Party Congress is still to come. I look forward to meeting the Polish leader when I go to the seaside next month. I wonder if he will be a Communist.


85. EXT. SEA SHORE. DAY

*This is the same shot as scene 1. The beach and the sea. Everything is the same except that* KANIA *has replaced* GIEREK.

NARRATOR: (*Voice over*) In August 1981 Stanislaw Kania, First Secretary of the Polish United Workers' Party, left Warsaw for his annual holiday in the Soviet Union by the Black Sea. There he met Leonid Brezhnev, First Secretary of the

Communist Party of the Soviet Union.
(*The two men, in hats, coats and lace-up shoes come together and embrace.*)
In an atmosphere of cordiality and complete mutual understanding the two leaders had a frank exchange of views.

86. EXT. SEASIDE. DAY

KANIA *and* BREZHNEV *are now in beach clothes, wearing sunglasses, straw hats and so on. A nervous* WAITER *is hovering with a tray of brightly coloured drinks.*

NARRATOR: (*Voice over*) The July Congress of the Polish United Workers' Party was over. It had been the first ever Communist Party Congress to be composed of freely elected delegates – 2,000 of them, mostly there for the first time. They started by voting in a Central Committee which swept aside seven-eighths of the old guard including four Politburo members. Kania, the great reformer, was re-elected First Secretary. Even so, the Congress knew that Poland was on the horns of a dilemma, and both horns made a showing in the Politburo. The hard-liner, Olszowski, made it to the top again.

BREZHNEV: Why did they keep Olszowski?

KANIA: He is respected for his economic ideas.

BREZHNEV: Why?

KANIA: Because Gierek sacked him.

BREZHNEV: And Jaruzelski?

KANIA: The Prime Minister is respected by all sides.
(*Suddenly irritated by the* WAITER, BREZHNEV *knocks the tray of drinks out of his hand.*)

BREZHNEV: (*Shouts*) Respect! (*Jabs a finger at* KANIA.) Do you know how you got into this mess?

KANIA: Comrade First Secretary, we must have strayed from the Leninist path . . .

BREZHNEV: You got into this mess by getting into debt to capitalist bankers!

87. INT. THE BANKERS' MEETING. DAY
*The set-up is much the same as the first bankers' meeting (scene 19).*

FINANSKY *is in the chair.*

FINANSKY: This is very harsh.

AMERICAN BANKER: I'm sorry but last March you had the unhappy distinction of being the first Communist country to request a rescheduling of its debts.

FINANSKY: We know what to do. Prices must increase two or three times over. A loaf of bread should perhaps quadruple. We know that. But you understand, we have problems.


88. EXT. STEELWORKS. DAY

*Top shot. Meeting of fifty workers being addressed by a* PARTY MAN.

NARRATOR: (*Voice over*) The Government announced food price increases of 123 per cent. There were daily disturbances. At workers' meetings when Party officials used the word –
(*Close up on* PARTY MAN *addressing the meeting.*)

PARTY MAN: Comrades!
(*He is greeted by sustained whistles of derision from the meeting.*)


89. INT. SOLIDARITY MEETING HALL. DAY

RAKOWSKI *is present with* WALESA *and a* SOLIDARITY TEAM, *including the* KATOWICE MAN *and a* MINER.

RAKOWSKI: The attitude of Solidarity is arrogant and offensive. You won't get eggs if you don't feed the chickens. Production this year is down 18 per cent. Coal is down 14 per cent. Wages are up 20 per cent.

MINER: I'm a coal miner, Comrade Rakowski. Miners are going to work hungry – how can you expect hungry men to raise production?

KATOWICE MAN: We're pouring steel to 40 per cent of capacity. The whole place is run inefficiently. We could double output if we had workers' self-management.

RAKOWSKI: For God's sake – one thing at a time.

WALESA: We don't have time. You've *had* time. It's almost exactly a year since we signed the agreement in Gdansk. We are cheated, lied to, misrepresented in the press and on TV. We've given you time. Next week we'll call a printers' strike. We'll close down TV and radio if we don't get the access we were promised.

RAKOWSKI: Are we here to talk about bread or TV?

MINER: Bread?

RAKOWSKI: I have to tell you from September 1st a loaf costing
seven zlotys will cost seventeen zlotys. Flour will increase
somewhat less. It will double.

(*The* SOLIDARITY MEN *look at each other silently and then get
up.*)

WALESA: We are not a poor country. We are badly managed.
The question of workers' councils to take charge of
production is now urgent.

MINER: (*To* WALESA) Gierek gave us those in '71. They soon got
sucked under by the Party machine.

WALESA: In '71 there was no Solidarity.

(WALESA *and his* COLLEAGUES *turn and walk out of the meeting
hall.*)

NARRATOR: (*Voice over*) On September 4th, the Soviet Union
put 100,000 men into military manoeuvres around Poland.
The following day the First National Congress of the Free
Independent Union Solidarity opened in a sports stadium in
Gdansk.


90. INT. SOLIDARITY CONGRESS. DAY

*The cut is to a big close up of* WALESA *addressing a large gathering.*

WALESA: . . . this Congress is the heritage of the blood of 1956,
of 1970, of 1976 and of all the struggles of the Polish
workers. The fight has only just begun but we shall win!

(WALESA *acknowledges sustained applause.*)

NARRATOR: (*Voice over*) The Congress called for free elections to
parliament, for union supervision of food production and
distribution, for public control of the mass media, for
workers' self-management. Jan Rulewski called for . . .

(*Mix to close up on* RULEWSKI.)

RULEWSKI: . . . deletion of the clause recognizing the leading
role of the Polish United Workers' Party . . .

(*There is a cut to* WALESA *listening. He shakes his head.*)

NARRATOR: (*Voice over*) There was worse to come.


91. INT. KANIA'S OFFICE. DAY

KANIA *and* JARUZELSKI *are present. The* INTERCOM *on the desk starts to announce,* His Excellency the Soviet Ambassador *but the furious* AMBASSADOR *is in the room waving a piece of paper before the* INTERCOM *has finished.*

AMBASSADOR: I quote. 'The delegates assembled in Gdansk send *greetings and expressions of support* to workers of Albania, Bulgaria, Czechoslovakia, the German Democratic Republic, Romania, Hungary and all nations of the Soviet Union . . . we share the same destiny . . . despite the lies disseminated in your countries . . . we support those of you who embark on the struggle for a free union movement . . .' I am ordered to make the strongest possible protest, on behalf of the Government of the Soviet Union.

KANIA: Of course. Thank you. I agree it is most regrettable.
(*The* AMBASSADOR *waits for more but there is a pause. In the end the* AMBASSADOR *nods a farewell and leaves the room.* KANIA *and* JARUZELSKI *look at each other.* JARUZELSKI *begins to laugh quietly.*)

JARUZELSKI: Albania. . . ! (*He finds this very funny.*) . . . Albania. . . !


92. INT. CAFE. NIGHT

WITNESS *and* NARRATOR.

WITNESS: It's not really funny. It's probably the end.

NARRATOR: No, they're still talking.
(*To camera*) During all this, the Government offered Solidarity a formula for workers' self-management. Evidently, they were still Poles talking to Poles.

WITNESS: Jaruzelski did his officer training in the Soviet Union.

NARRATOR: (*To camera*) During all this, the Government offered Solidarity a formula for workers' management. Evidently, the Party was playing cat and mouse with the union.


93. INT. MOVING FIAT CAR. NIGHT

WALESA *is driving.* RULEWSKI *is next to him. Two* SOLIDARITY MEMBERS *sit in the back.*

WALESA: (*To* RULEWSKI) Jan, stick to Poland. Let the Albanians and the Hungarians and the Bulgarians look after themselves. I'm surprised Rakowski is still talking to us. How are the others getting there?

RULEWSKI: It's just us four.

WALESA: That's just how I like it. A praesidium that can fit into a Fiat.

94. INT. SOLIDARITY CONGRESS. DAY

JURCZYK *is addressing a large audience.*

JURCZYK: I move that we reprimand Lech Walesa and his Praesidium colleagues for the undemocratic way in which they reached this decision on workers' self-management. Four men voted three to one, and they presumed to overturn a resolution made by 900 of us in this hall!

WALESA: (*In close up – shouting*) We could have come back empty-handed! But we didn't, we made a decision. It takes no guts at all to stand up here and complain about the world.

95. INT. OFFICE (SOLIDARITY CONGRESS). DAY

WALESA *lies exhausted across three chairs.* RULEWSKI *walks across and looks down at him.*

RULEWSKI: I'm standing against you for the leadership.

WALESA: You're making a mistake, Jan.

RULEWSKI: Why? Do you think you're indispensable?

WALESA: No. But Marian Jurczyk is already standing against me. You'll split the vote.

RULEWSKI: Gwiazda is standing, too.

WALESA: The three of you. All or nothing. Now or never. I've been trying to tell you for a year. That's how to lose. (WALESA *puts his head back and closes his eyes.* RULEWSKI *watches him for a moment and then turns and leaves. The office furniture, television sets etc., are being cleared away around* WALESA. *Bulletin boards are being taken off the walls. Files are being stacked.* WALESA *sleeps on.*)

NARRATOR: (*Voice over*) Walesa won with 55 per cent of the vote. Marian Jurczyk polled 24 per cent, Andrzej Gwiazda 9 per cent, and Jan Rulewski 6 per cent. The delegates left the floor of the rented sports hall which was then flooded and frozen over for a hockey game.

96. INT. A DRESSING ROOM. DAY

*In fact we could be anywhere because the scene is of crisp separate close ups on a man* (JARUZELSKI) *putting on a military uniform, the belt, the hat, etc.*

NARRATOR: (*Voice over*) Talks began again between Solidarity and the Government. The union gave the Government ten days to produce results or face a national strike. Within a week there was a result of sorts.

*(The last article to be donned is the pair of tinted glasses worn by* JARUZELSKI.)

97. INT. FIRST SECRETARY'S OFFICE. DAY

*A* SECRETARY (*a man*) *is arranging files on the otherwise empty desk.* JARUZELSKI *walks into the room.*

SECRETARY: Good morning, Comrade First Secretary. Everything is ready for you.

JARUZELSKI: Thank you.

(JARUZELSKI *goes to sit behind the desk.*)

NARRATOR: (*Voice over*) For the first time in a Communist country one man was head of the Party, the government and the army. It was the first Communist Party anywhere to be led by a general.

(JARUZELSKI *sits down, looks around, pleased, and gives his uniform a little flick.*)

JARUZELSKI: You don't think the effect is . . . a bit South American?

# Part Four: The General

98. EXT. PARADE GROUND. DAY

*The cut is to a close up of* GENERAL JARUZELSKI.

NARRATOR: (*Voice over*) Back in August, the General said . . .

JARUZELSKI: (*Declaiming*) How long can the patience,
moderation and good will of the Republic be put to the
test? Polish soldiers have the right to say: enough of this
indulgence!

(*We cut to the* GENERAL *reviewing a line of* YOUNG OFFICERS.)

NARRATOR: The fact that he was speaking to a passing-out
parade of young officers at the time made it less startling
than it might have been . . . but nowadays there were
generals in more and more government posts – education,
money, transport, even a general in charge of the Polish
airline. The only thing missing was the appointment of the
Chief of the General Staff to the Politburo and that came at
the end of October.

99. INT. WALESA FLAT. EVENING

WALESA *and his wife* DANUTA *and six* CHILDREN *are eating at a
table big enough for them and two guests,* KURON *and* GWIAZDA
DANUTA *is pregnant.*

KURON: I think political rule in Poland is already a sort of
fiction. The army is starting to run things. *Political* power is
lying in the gutter for somebody to pick up. Maybe the
people nearest the gutter have the best chance – the
Stalinists who call it socialism, the anti-Semites who call it
nationalism . . . *You* have no chance at all. If you were
handed power on a plate you'd be left fighting over the
plate. I thought a workers' protest movement could lead to
a truly socialist Poland. It required discipline and stability.
It required solidarity. The union executive is being pulled

82

around like a tin can tied to a dog's tail.

GWIAZDA: We deserve it. The workers are activists, we're a bureaucracy.

WALESA: How else are we supposed to negotiate for them?

GWIAZDA: We negotiate, they fight.

WALESA: That's surrender. Not to the Government, to chaos. I'm going to propose a national warning strike so that at least for an hour we look like an organization again.

GWIAZDA: (*Exploding*) Jesus Christ! In Katowice there were 5,000 fighting the police with stones! Students took over the radio station! And you want to stop work for lunch!

WALESA: That's right!

(*It has become a loud row.*)

I don't want 5,000 people throwing stones somewhere at the other end of the country. It produces nothing except an opportunity for the generals who can't wait to save the nation.

(*To* KURON) I'm right, aren't I?

(KURON *gets up.*)

KURON: I'm going back to Warsaw. We have to start again.

WALESA: A new party?

KURON: No. A reappraisal.

GWIAZDA: A discussion group. Maybe you can write another open letter.

KURON: (*Losing his temper, too*) The Communist Manifesto was an open letter! The written word – I believe in it. When this tower of Babel collapses upon itself you'll need to be reminded what the noise was all about.

(*This takes him to the door.*)

(*More quietly*) You failed because you had no reliable framework for your actions. If you want freedom of action in a Communist state the strategy will have to be thought out better than this. Maybe it will have to be the intellectuals after all. Next time, eh?

(KURON *leaves. After a pause* WALESA *also gets up from the table and leaves, into another room, closing the door.*)

GWIAZDA: (*To* DANUTA) I'm going.

(DANUTA *nods.*)

Thank you.

(GWIAZDA *leaves the flat.*)

### 100. EXT. PLAYGROUND. DAY

*The* NARRATOR *is there watching several of the* WALESA CHILDREN *playing with a ball.*

FIRST CHILD: Poor Mr Kuron . . .

SECOND CHILD: He thinks if he leaves the Party alone . . .

THIRD CHILD: . . . the Party will leave him alone.

FIRST CHILD: Poor Mr Kuron.

WITNESS: (*Voice over*) A cheap trick, in my opinion . . . Out of the mouths of children . . .

### 101. INT. CAFE

*The* NARRATOR *and the* WITNESS *are drinking together. The* WITNESS *is still speaking.*

WITNESS: . . . Why didn't you give them a puppy to make sure?

NARRATOR: Do the Walesas have a dog?

WITNESS: It's a little late to be scrupulous about detail.

NARRATOR: What's the answer to Kuron?

WITNESS: I know Kuron. In 1800 he was in nostalgic exile in Paris waiting for history to put the clock back. In 1900 he was a revolutionary Marxist in London waiting for the proletariat to put the clock forward. Now he's in People's Poland and it seems to be neither one thing nor the other, an independent slave-state ruled by worker-princes. No wonder he's disappointed.

NARRATOR: Well, then what. . . ?

WITNESS: He's got it upside down, in my opinion. Theories don't guarantee social justice, social justice tells you if a theory is any good. Right and wrong are not complicated – when a child cries, 'That's not fair!' the child can be believed. Children are always right. But it was still a cheap trick.

NARRATOR: I'll take it back.

### 102. INT. WALESA FLAT. EVENING

*As before. The scene has got to the point where* KURON *is at the door, about to leave.*

KURON: Next time, eh?

(*To* WALESA) I think your plan is good. Get the best deal you can for the working man. You're a union, after all.

103. INT. STEELWORKS. DAY
WALESA *is in the foreground. Low camera angle.* WORKERS *are in the gantry above. The factory is loud and busy.*
WALESA *looks at his watch. At that moment the sirens sound.*

104. INT. OPERATIONS ROOM. DAY
*There is a map table and maps and city plans on the walls. Half a dozen high-ranking* MILITARY OFFICERS *are crowded round the table.* JARUZELSKI *is among them, using a pointer to indicate different parts of the map. The siren sound overlaps with diminished volume, into this room. The* ARMY OFFICERS *all pause and look up, listening . . .*

105. INT. STEELWORKS. DAY
WALESA *is where he was. The siren is just finishing. The machinery is coming to a halt. So are the men who were working.*
WALESA: It's music to them . . . music . . .

106. INT. PARLIAMENT. DAY
JARUZELSKI *is at the microphone.*
JARUZELSKI: In the Central Committee, even in the Politburo, there are voices asking us to set our democratic system aside until peace is restored. What I will ask of this assembly is to prepare itself for a situation where I will have to come to you and ask for emergency laws. There are 12,000 on strike in the textile mills. If the independent union cannot control its anarchists, we will have to find some other way . . .

107. INT. GOVERNMENT MEETING ROOM. DAY
*On one side of the large table is* RAKOWSKI *flanked by two* ADVISERS. *He is faced by* WALESA *similarly attended.*
WALESA: I was in the textile mills. I have met these anarchists . . . 12,000 women, young girls and grannies, working wives . . . Do you think they're on strike because they want to overthrow the Party? No, they're on strike because work brings no reward, and it doesn't look as if the Government knows what to do about it. They get up in the

85

dark to stand in line for hours to buy a pair of shoes the wrong size so that they may have something to barter for a piece of meat – which turns out to be rotten. They appeal to you, and you say – oh, we can't help it, these anarchists are making life impossible. And then it turns out *they're* the anarchists! Listen, they can't break the circle, someone else has to. I don't think you can do it on your own.

RAKOWSKI: I agree. You know our proposal – an action front representing all the social forces – the Government, Solidarity, the Church, the peasants, the official unions, Catholic intellectuals, economists, scientists – a team of national unity –

WALESA: You just want to water us down. But we're 10 million and we won't sit down as equal partners with the incompetents and hacks – the central planners, the time-servers, the seat warmers – all the ones who had the chance and lost it. You've failed, and the best answer now is an economic council, independent, with real power, made up of Solidarity and Government equally with equal voices.

RAKOWSKI: (*Angrily*) What sort of government do you expect to hand over its authority to a committee?

WALESA: Your sort. A government with no mandate at the end of its string.

(RAKOWSKI, *insulted, gets up from the table and walks away, perhaps towards a window. His* ADVISERS *look stonily across the table.* WALESA *and the* SOLIDARITY MEN *stand up and prepare to leave.*)

RAKOWSKI: Perhaps you'd like to tell that to the General?

WALESA: (*With conscious irony*) Do you mean the Prime Minister?

RAKOWSKI: Yes, the Prime Minister. The First Secretary. The General.

WALESA: How many votes does he get?


108. INT. POLITBURO VESTIBULE. DAY

*The* SOLIDARITY TEAM *is leaving.* RAKOWSKI *appears.*

RAKOWSKI: Comrade Walesa –

(WALESA *drops back.* RAKOWSKI *takes him aside. He speaks quietly.*)

General Jaruzelski is interested in a new initiative. With
Archbishop Glemp. Will you meet them?

WALESA: Just the three of us?

RAKOWSKI: Just the three of you.

109. INT. SOLIDARITY MEETING ROOM (GDANSK). DAY

*There are four men in the room . . . WALESA, GWIAZDA, RULEWSKI
and JURCZYK. Because of the size of the room, some of the
conversation may be shouted across the yards of space.*

RULEWSKI: What do they want? Your autograph?

GWIAZDA: You had no authority to accept.

WALESA: Should we announce that we aren't even willing to talk
to the Prime Minister and the Primate of Poland?

GWIAZDA: Not we, you. Why you?

WALESA: I was asked.

GWIAZDA: You were asked because you're Jaruzelski's meat.
You're a babe in arms.

RULEWSKI: So is Glemp. The General wants the moral authority
of the Church and the social seal of approval of Solidarity.

GWIAZDA: They'll muzzle you.

WALESA: I'm going.

GWIAZDA: Lech, you're a vain fool! Your moustache is famous
but there is nothing above it.

WALESA: (*Over the top*) You can throw me out any time you like.
I'll go and I'll take the union with me. I'll dissolve it inside
two weeks!

(*The others look at each other in astonishment.*)

RULEWSKI: Where will you take it? To New York? In two weeks
you will be the guest of the American unions. Maybe you
should have taken the union with you when you went to
Geneva – to Japan – to Paris – to the Vatican.

JURCZYK: We don't have to destroy ourselves, there's others
willing to do it –

WALESA: Yes, that's right, Marian – and one way to destroy us is
to go round making speeches calling the Government
traitors, Moscow's servants, Jews – what did you mean by
it?

JURCZYK: I meant they're traitors, Moscow's servants and in
some cases Jews.

WALESA:  As a Catholic I reject you, as a union we dissociate ourselves from such talk.

JURCZYK:  Wait till you get to America. The Americans won't hear a word you say about your ideals for socialism – they'll make an anti-Russian carnival out of you.

(WALESA's *manner changes instantly as he takes this in.*)

WALESA:  That's true. You're right. I won't go. The American trip is off. As of now.

(*The other three are astonished by him again.*)

(*Smiles.*) That's right. When somebody's right they don't have to argue with me. The right move and the wrong move – I don't need arguments. I can feel it – right and wrong. The meeting feels right, and I'm going to it.


110. INT. GOVERNMENT GUEST HOUSE. EVENING

*There is a green baize card table and three chairs. The* NARRATOR *is standing by, shuffling a pack of cards.*

NARRATOR:  (*To camera*) Cardinal Wyszynski had died in May. The new Primate of Poland was Archbishop Joseph Glemp. The meeting which took place between the Primate, the General and the union leader on November 4th 1981 was without precedent, not just in the Polish crisis but in the Communist world. It lasted 2 hours and 20 minutes.

(*The* NARRATOR *starts to deal the cards three ways.*)

That much is known. But as to who said what to whom . . .

(*The* WITNESS *appears with a carafe and three glasses. He puts them on the table.*)

WITNESS:  Don't tell me, let me guess. Cards on the table.

NARRATOR:  Playing one's hand.

WITNESS:  Writers.


111. INT. THE SAME. EVENING

*There is the card table and the three chairs, with a hand of cards waiting at each place.* JARUZELSKI, GLEMP *and* WALESA *approach the table and sit down. Each looks at his own cards. The three men play cards as they speak. They pick up and put down cards as it becomes their turn to speak. The cards are seen to be not conventional. Their designs, in red and white, show, variously, the Polish Eagle, a Church symbol, the Solidarity symbol, the hammer and sickle . . . but there is no attempt to make the rules of the game precisely intelligible to the audience. The impression is that the game is a form of whist.*

JARUZELSKI: We are Poles. There is much we can agree on.

GLEMP: Certainly we want to settle our own problems.

WALESA: All right.

JARUZELSKI: Thank you.

(JARUZELSKI *picks up the three cards as a 'trick'. He puts down a card.*)

The Russians are reluctant to intervene but at a certain point they would have to overcome their reluctance. That point will be reached when socialism breaks down in this country.

GLEMP: I agree.

WALESA: We can't even agree on language. What is this socialism you're talking about? Solidarity is socialism.

JARUZELSKI: It is not Lenin's socialism.

GLEMP: Let us say that Solidarity is socialism. But is it not breaking down? Socialism is order. (*To* WALESA) Your extremists create disorder.

WALESA: (*Upset*) Father, the Government is trying to make accomplices of us by holding these Russians over our heads – 'Behave yourselves for Poland's sake!' Why should we believe it? I don't think the Russians can afford to intervene.

JARUZELSKI: They can never afford to until they can't afford not to.

(*He picks up the second 'trick'.*)

The Polish Church is unique, a stronghold of Christianity in the Communist world. Soviet intervention would change many things.

GLEMP: Not just for the Church. It would certainly be the end of the free trade unions.

WALESA: The Russian scare shouldn't change what we think or do. That's blackmail and it's not moral to give in to it. We can afford to be wrong but the Church has got to be right.

(WALESA *stands up abruptly, throwing down his cards. The picture freezes.*)

NARRATOR: (*Voice over*) But there was no fly on the wall. No one

knows how little help Walesa got from Archbishop Glemp.
Or how much.

(*The scene cuts back to the beginning, the game beginning
again.*)

JARUZELSKI:  We are Poles. There is much we can agree on.

GLEMP:  Certainly we want to settle our own problems.

WALESA:  All right.

JARUZELSKI:  Thank you.

(JARUZELSKI *picks up the 'trick'.*)

The Russians are reluctant to intervene but they would
have to overcome their reluctance if socialism breaks down
in this country.

GLEMP:  (*Turning on* JARUZELSKI) We can't even agree on
language. What is this intervention? It is invasion and
occupation to rescue a discredited dictatorship!

WALESA:  (*Cautiously*) But invasion would change many things,
not just for the union. The Polish Church has a unique
position and it has been won at great sacrifice.

JARUZELSKI:  The dictatorship of the proletariat as expressed
through the Party is the only government we've got and
Solidarity is not letting it govern.

GLEMP:  (*Again attacking* JARUZELSKI) The Government has
reneged on most of the provisions of the Gdansk
Agreement. The conflict is of your creation because you
deny the rights of the citizen!

(*The picture freezes again.*)

NARRATOR:  (*Voice over*) Everything is true except the words and
the pictures. It wasn't a card game.

(*The scene cuts back to the beginning but now it is not a card
game. The table is polished wood.*)

But time was running out. There were to be elections in
February and the one problem a Communist government
cannot afford is to get re-elected.

JARUZELSKI:  We have elections in February. (*To* WALESA) You
proclaimed a trade union with no interest in politics. In the
last few months, thirty-five anti-socialist groups posing as
political parties have been formed. We all have reason to
fear the consequences. The Russians are reluctant to
intervene but at a certain point they will have to overcome

their reluctance.

GLEMP: Poland's socialist dictatorship is the most democratic government we've got, and the most Polish. We are here to decide how we can best help it clothe and feed the population. Am I wrong? Without the economic problem there would be no political problem. Without the political problem there would be no Russian problem.

WALESA: No, you're not wrong.

JARUZELSKI: We have coal reserves for two more weeks. How do I get the country running again? (*To* WALESA) I've asked you to ban wildcat strikes. I've offered to sit down with you in a council for national renewal.

WALESA: With us and enough others to give you a tame majority.

GLEMP: What if Solidarity had a veto?

JARUZELSKI: No. But perhaps if every member had the right of veto . . .

WALESA: No.

JARUZELSKI: Then just Solidarity and the Government.

GLEMP: And the Church.

JARUZELSKI: That's possible. (*To* WALESA) What do you say? (*Pause.*)

WALESA: There's a meeting tonight of the Solidarity National Commission, I have to go back to Gdansk.


II2. INT. SOLIDARITY NATIONAL COMMISSION. NIGHT

*The meeting is noisy. The familiar faces are there.* GWIAZDA *is in the chair.* WALESA (*dressed as for the Glemp/Jaruzelski meeting*) *appears.* GWIAZDA *sees him.*

GWIAZDA: Lech!

(*The meeting goes quiet.*)

We didn't wait. We've made some progress.

WALESA: I've got something to put to the vote.

GWIAZDA: We already voted. A national strike in three months if the Government doesn't satisfy conditions.

WALESA: And a ban on unofficial strikes?

GWIAZDA: We voted on that too. No ban.

WALESA: Is that your idea of progress?

GWIAZDA: Yes. It is.

(WALESA *approaches him.*)

WALESA: You're sitting in my chair.

(GWIAZDA *vacates the chair.* WALESA *takes it. He picks up the microphone in front of him.*)

If it's confrontation you want, that's fine because that's what you're voting for. You might as well leave now and start prising up the cobbles off the streets.

(*The meeting goes quiet for him.*)

I'm here with a new formula for talking with the Government – a national committee of –

(*The meeting starts murmuring against him.*)

Yes, I know. They lie. They cheat. They kick and bite and scratch before they give an inch – but that's how we got this union, inch by inch across the negotiating table!

(*The meeting starts to applaud, a slow build interrupted by* GWIAZDA.)

GWIAZDA: (*Shouting*) We got it by going on strike and staying on strike.

WALESA: You're wrong. We got it because we could deliver a return to work. We've got nothing else to negotiate with, and if we can't deliver, what have they got to lose?

(*The applause grows.*)

GWIAZDA: They've conned you, Lech! The talks are a sham. Across the table is where they want us – all the time we're talking they're getting ready to hit us. You keep the chair – I'm not going to be needing it.

(GWIAZDA *leaves and from different places about a dozen men, ones who were not clapping, leave with him.*)

113. EXT. PLAYGROUND (GDANSK). DAY

WALESA *and his* WIFE *and* CHILDREN *are in the playground. The* CHILDREN *are running around at some distance and playing.* (DANUTA *is pregnant.*)

WALESA: Andrzej's resigned. Him and others. They say my line is too soft. Maybe it is. I read in the papers that Walesa is a moderate and Gwiazda is a radical and I feel a sort of shame. How brave it sounds, to be a radical.

DANUTA: You're radical enough. Solidarity is losing its halo, Lech. The TV makes you look like saboteurs. You're getting blamed for the shortages, for the farmers' strikes, the student strikes, the taxi drivers' strike . . . for everything. People are saying the Government can't solve it, Solidarity can't solve it, there's only the army left, and better ours than theirs.

WALESA: What people?

DANUTA: Ordinary people. You know. Not the Praesidium. Not the Government. People.

WALESA: I wish I could talk to Jacek.

DANUTA: Why can't you?


114. INT. POLICE CELL. DAY

*The* WITNESS, *the worse for wear, is flung into the cell.* KURON *is lying on a bunk in the cell.*

WITNESS: Where did they get you?

KURON: At home.

WITNESS: What for?

KURON: Attempting to overthrow the state. I think. What's happening outside?

WITNESS: The fire brigade cadets have taken over the college.

KURON: Strikers in uniform? Well, we're getting there.


115. INT. OPERATIONS ROOM. DAY

JARUZELSKI *has a visitor* – MARSHAL KULIKOV.

JARUZELSKI: We're getting there. The Western bankers have given us an ultimatum, the zloty is being devalued, and parliament won't pass a strike law. I would say . . . about a week. Tomorrow we move in against the fire brigade cadets.

KULIKOV: Troops?

JARUZELSKI: (*Shaking his head*) Not yet. Riot police. We'll use helicopters to secure the roof and go in through the main gate.


116. EXT. STREET

*There is a lot of noise. There is a helicopter noise overhead.* WALESA *is there looking up. He is joined by a furious and triumphant* GWIAZDA.

GWIAZDA: And you're still talking to them about workers' self-management! It's confrontation, Lech.

WALESA: Yes. I know.


117. INT. SOLIDARITY MEETING ROOM. DAY

*This is a meeting of about twenty people, the Praesidium and Regional Chairmen of Solidarity.* WALESA *is speaking.*

WALESA: Confrontation was always at the end of the road. I hoped to get there by easy stages. I think we could have got further, but I miscalculated. So we have to change our tactics and be prepared to move at lightning speed.

BUJAK: We'll liberate the radio and TV . . . we'll establish our own council for the national economy. It will be like a provisional government.


118. INT. JARUZELSKI'S OFFICE. DAY

JARUZELSKI *is listening to a tape of Bujak's speech.*

BUJAK: (*On tape*) . . . we'll establish our own council for the national economy. It will be like a provisional government.

JARUZELSKI: We're there.

(*We see that he is talking to* MARSHAL KULIKOV.)

KULIKOV: None too soon. This trap has been a long time springing.

JARUZELSKI: Forgive me, Marshal, we prefer to think of it as a regrettable outcome.

KULIKOV: We all forgive you, Wojciech.


119. INT. WALESA BEDROOM. NIGHT

DANUTA *is in bed.* WALESA *enters without putting on the light. He sits on the bed and starts taking his shoes off.*

NARRATOR: (*Voice over*) The final meeting of the National Commission of Solidarity ended in Gdansk on Saturday night, December 12th. There was going to be a national day of protest, a general strike against strike laws, and, going all the way now, a reappraisal of the Soviet connection.

DANUTA: Remember once they arrested you when I was nearly giving birth? Which baby was that?

WALESA: Yes, I remember. Everything was simpler then. We didn't fight amongst ourselves. There was only one way to go. Then round the corner there was a fork in the road, and each fork led to a fork . . . so we got separated. Well, it's been sixteen months. We've gone further and quicker than anyone expected. Jacek said we could win little by little, or lose overnight.

DANUTA: Lech. . . ?

WALESA: They've cut the phone lines from Gdansk. I'm sorry. We may be apart for a while.

DANUTA: You don't know that. Lech. . . ?

WALESA: I think I've always known.

### 120. INT. POLICE CELL. NIGHT

*The* WITNESS *is asleep.* KURON *apparently doesn't know it, for he is pacing the cell, talking angrily.*

KURON: It was not a conflict between ideologies – trying to make one system fit in with another. (*Scornfully*) Marxist-Leninism! – what would Lenin have thought of the Polish Church? Or Polish agriculture – 80 per cent privately owned. Ideology is as dead as Lenin. All Brezhnev demanded from us was a political guarantee of the military alliance, and reliable railways for the army. All the rest is self-delusion.

### 121. INT. AIRFIELD. NIGHT

*There is a parked helicopter with its rotors spinning.* WALESA *is escorted into the helicopter which then takes flight.*

NARRATOR: (*Voice over*) By dawn on Sunday, December 13th, almost the entire Solidarity leadership was under arrest. The military council which announced itself as Poland's saviour also arrested the former First Secretary, Edward Gierek, together with five others who had helped him to bring the Party and the country to the point in August 1980 when the shipyard workers on the Baltic Coast went on strike and demanded the right to form a free and independent trade union.

### 122. EXT. SEA SHORE. DAY

*The beach and sea again. Everything is the same except that* JARUZELSKI *has replaced* KANIA.

NARRATOR: (*Voice over*) When the summer came, Wojciech

Jaruzelski, First Secretary of the Polish United Workers'
Party, left Warsaw for his holiday in the Soviet Union by
the Black Sea. There he met Leonid Brezhnev, First
Secretary of the Communist Party of the Soviet Union.
(BREZHNEV *approaches, and the two men come together and
embrace.*)
In an atmosphere of cordiality and complete mutual
understanding the two leaders had a frank exchange of
views.

BREZHNEV: Greetings, Comrade!

JARUZELSKI: Greetings, Comrade First Secretary!

BREZHNEV: So, how's tricks?

JARUZELSKI: Fine.

BREZHNEV: And Mrs Jaruzelski?

JARUZELSKI: Who? – oh, fine. And you?

BREZHNEV: To tell you the truth, I haven't been feeling too well.

    (*They walk together up the beach.*)

# EVERY GOOD BOY DESERVES FAVOUR

A Play for Actors and Orchestra

To Victor Fainberg and Vladimir Bukovsky

## Characters

Although in this edition only the text is printed, *Every Good Boy Deserves Favour* is a work consisting of words and music, and is incomplete without the score composed by its co-author André Previn.

*Every Good Boy Deserves Favour* was first performed at the Festival Hall in July 1977, with the London Symphony Orchestra, conducted by André Previn. The cast was as follows:

| | |
|---|---|
| ALEXANDER | Ian McKellen |
| IVANOV | John Wood |
| SACHA | Andrew Sheldon |
| DOCTOR | Patrick Stewart |
| TEACHER | Barbara Leigh-Hunt |
| COLONEL | Philip Locke |
| | |
| Director | Trevor Nunn |
| Designer | Ralph Koltai |

*Three separate acting areas are needed.*
  1. *The* CELL *needs two beds.*
  2. *The* OFFICE *needs a table and two chairs.*
  3. *The* SCHOOL *needs a school desk.*
*These areas can be as small as possible but each has to be approachable from each of the others, and the lighting on each ought to be at least partly controllable independently of the other two and of the orchestra itself, which needless to say occupies the platform.*

*The* CELL *is occupied by two men,* ALEXANDER *amd* IVANOV. ALEXANDER *is a political prisoner and* IVANOV *is a genuine mental patient.*

*It will become clear in performance, but may well be stated now, that the orchestra for part of the time exists in the imagination of* IVANOV. IVANOV *has with him an orchestral triangle.*

*The* OFFICE *is empty.*

*In the* SCHOOL *the* TEACHER *stands, and* SACHA *sits at the desk.*

CELL

*The* OFFICE *and* SCHOOL *are not 'lit'. In the* CELL, ALEXANDER *and* IVANOV *sit on their respective beds. The orchestra tunes-up. The tuning-up continues normally but after a minute or two the musicians lapse into miming the tuning-up.*

*Thus we have silence while the orchestra goes through the motions of tuning.*

IVANOV *stands up, with his triangle and rod. The orchestra becomes immobile.*

*Silence.*

IVANOV *strikes the triangle, once. The orchestra starts miming a performance. He stands concentrating, listening to music which we cannot hear, and striking his triangle as and when the 'music' requires it. We only hear the triangle occasionally.* ALEXANDER *watches this—a man watching another man occasionally hitting a triangle.*

*This probably lasts under a minute. Then, very quietly, we begin to hear what* IVANOV *can hear, i.e. the orchestra becomes audible. So now his striking of the triangle begins to fit into the context which makes sense of it.*

*The music builds slowly, gently. And then on a single cue the platform light level jumps up with the conductor in position and the orchestra playing fully and loudly. The triangle is a prominent part in the symphony.*

*Now we are flying.* ALEXANDER *just keeps watching* IVANOV.


IVANOV: (*Furiously interrupts*) —No—no—no—
    (*The orchestra drags to a halt.*)
    (*Shouts.*) Go back to the timpani.
    (*The orchestra goes back, then relapses progressively, swiftly, into mime, and when it is almost inaudible* ALEXANDER *coughs loudly.* IVANOV *glances at him reproachfully. After the cough there is only silence with* IVANOV *intermittently striking his triangle, and the orchestra miming.*)
IVANOV: Better—good—much better . . .
    (ALEXANDER *is trying not to cough.*
    IVANOV *finishes with a final beat on the triangle.*
    *The orchestra finishes.*
    IVANOV *sits down.* ALEXANDER *coughs luxuriously.*)
IVANOV: (*Apologetically*) I know what you're thinking.
ALEXANDER: (*Understandingly*) It's all right.
IVANOV: No, you can say it. The cellos are rubbish.
ALEXANDER: (*Cautiously*) I'm not really a judge of music.
IVANOV: I was scraping the bottom of the barrel, and that's how they sound. And what about the horns?—should I persevere with them?
ALEXANDER: The horns?
IVANOV: Brazen to a man but mealy-mouthed. Butter wouldn't melt. When I try to reason with them they purse their lips. Tell me, do you have an opinion on the fungoid log-rollers spreading wet rot through the woodwinds? Not to speak of the glockenspiel.
ALEXANDER: The glockenspiel?
IVANOV: I asked you not to speak of it. Give me a word for the harpist.

ALEXANDER: I don't really—

IVANOV: Plucky. A harpist who rushes in where a fool would fear to tread—with all my problems you'd think I'd be spared exquisite irony. I've got a blue-arsed bassoon, a blue-tongued contra-bassoon, an organ grinder's chimpani, and the bass drum is in urgent need of a dermatologist.

ALEXANDER: Your condition is interesting.

IVANOV: I've got a violin section which is to violin playing what Heifetz is to water-polo. I've got a tubercular great-nephew of John Philip Sousa who goes oom when he should be going pah. And the Jew's harp has applied for a visa. I'm seriously thinking of getting a new orchestra. Do you read music?

ALEXANDER: No.

IVANOV: Don't worry: crochets, minims, sharp, flat, every good boy deserves favour. You'll pick it up in no time. What is your instrument?

ALEXANDER: I do not play an instrument.

IVANOV: Percussion? Strings? Brass?

ALEXANDER: No.

IVANOV: Reed? Keyboard?

ALEXANDER: I'm afraid not.

IVANOV: I'm amazed. Not keyboard. Wait a minute—flute.

ALEXANDER: No. Really.

IVANOV: Extraordinary. Give me a clue. If I beat you to a pulp would you try to protect your face or your hands? Which would be the more serious—if you couldn't sit down for a week or couldn't stand up? I'm trying to narrow it down, you see. Can I take it you don't stick this instrument up your arse in a kneeling position?

ALEXANDER: I do not play an instrument.

IVANOV: You can speak frankly. You will find I am without prejudice. I have invited musicians *into my own house*. And do you know why?—because we all have some musician in us. Any man says he has no musician in him, I'll call that man a *bigot*. Listen, I've had clarinet players eating *at my own table*. I've had French whores and gigolos speak to me in the *public street*, I mean horns, I mean piccolos, so don't worry about *me*, maestro, I've sat down with them, *drummers* even, sharing a plate of tagliatelle Verdi and stuffed Puccini

—why, I know people who make the orchestra eat in the kitchen, off scraps, the way you'd throw a trombone to a dog, I mean a second violinist, I mean to the lions; I love musicians, I respect them, human beings to a man. Let me put it like this: if I smashed this instrument of yours over your head, would you need a carpenter, a welder, or a brain surgeon?

ALEXANDER: I do not play an instrument. If I played an instrument I'd tell you what it was. But I do not play one. I have never played one. I do not know how to play one. I am not a musician.

IVANOV: What the hell are you doing here?

ALEXANDER: I was put here.

IVANOV: What for?

ALEXANDER: For slander.

IVANOV: Slander? What a fool! *Never speak ill of a musician!*— those bastards won't rest. They're animals, to a man.

ALEXANDER: This was political.

IVANOV: Let me give you some advice. Number one—never mix music with politics. Number two—never confide in your psychiatrist. Number three—*practise!*

ALEXANDER: Thank you.

(IVANOV *strikes his triangle once.*
*The* CELL *lighting fades.*
*Percussion band. The music is that of a band of young children. It includes strings but they are only plucked.*
*Pretty soon the percussion performance goes wrong because there is a subversive triangle in it. The triangle is struck randomly and then rapidly, until finally it is the only instrument to be heard. And then the triangle stops.*)


SCHOOL
*The lights come up on the* TEACHER *and* SACHA. *The* TEACHER *is holding a triangle.*

TEACHER: Well? Are you colour blind?

SACHA: No.

TEACHER: Let me see your music.

(SACHA *has sheet music on his desk.*)
Very well. What are the red notes?

SACHA: Strings.

TEACHER: Green?

SACHA: Tambourine.

TEACHER: Purple?

SACHA: Drum.

TEACHER: Yellow?

SACHA: Triangle.

TEACHER: Do you see forty yellow notes in a row?

SACHA: No.

TEACHER: What then? Detention is becoming a family tradition. Your name is notorious. Did you know that?

SACHA: Yes.

TEACHER: How did you know?

SACHA: Everybody tells me.

TEACHER: Open a book.

SACHA: What book?

TEACHER: Any book. *Fathers and Sons*, perhaps.

(SACHA *takes a book out of the desk.*)

Is it Turgenev?

SACHA: It's my geometry book.

TEACHER: Yes, your name goes round the world. By telegram. It is printed in the newspapers. It is spoken on the radio. With such a famous name why should you bother with different colours? We will change the music for you. It will look like a field of buttercups, and sound like dinnertime.

SACHA: I don't want to be in the orchestra.

TEACHER: Open the book. Pencil and paper. You see what happens to anti-social malcontents.

SACHA: Will I be sent to the lunatics' prison?

TEACHER: Certainly not. Read aloud.

SACHA: 'A point has position but no dimension.'

TEACHER: The asylum is for malcontents who don't know what they're doing.

SACHA: 'A line has length but no breadth.'

TEACHER: They know what they're doing but they don't know it's anti-social.

SACHA: 'A straight line is the shortest distance between two points.'

TEACHER: They know it's anti-social but they're fanatics.

SACHA: 'A circle is the path of a point moving equidistant to a given point.'

TEACHER: They're sick.

SACHA: 'A polygon is a plane area bounded by straight lines.'

TEACHER: And it's not a prison, it's a hospital.

(*Pause.*)

SACHA: 'A triangle is the polygon bounded by the fewest possible
sides.'

TEACHER: Good. Perfect. Copy neatly ten times, and if you're a
good boy I might find you a better instrument.

SACHA: (*Writing*) 'A triangle is the polygon bounded by the
fewest possible sides.' Is this what they make papa do?

TEACHER: Yes. They make him copy, 'I am a member of an
orchestra and we must play together.'

SACHA: How many times?

TEACHER: A million.

SACHA: A million?

(*Pause.*)

(*Cries.*) Papa!

ALEXANDER: (*Cries*) Sacha!

(*This cry is* ALEXANDER *shouting in his sleep at the other end of
the stage.*

IVANOV *sits watching* ALEXANDER.

*The orchestra plays chords between the following.*)

SACHA: Papa!

TEACHER: Hush!

ALEXANDER: Sacha!

(*The orchestra continues with percussion element for perhaps
ten seconds and then is sabotaged by a triangle beaten rapidly,
until the triangle is the only sound heard.*

ALEXANDER *sits up and the triangle stops.*)


CELL

IVANOV: Dinner time. (*Orchestra.*)


OFFICE

IVANOV *goes to sit at the table in the* OFFICE, *which is now the lit
area.*

*In the orchestra one of the lowliest violinists leaves his place. The
orchestra accompanies and parodies this man's actions as he leaves the*

*platform and enters the* OFFICE. IVANOV *is sitting at the table on one of the chairs. The man* (DOCTOR) *puts his violin on the table. The orchestra has been following him the whole time and the* DOCTOR's *movements fit precisely to the music.*

IVANOV *jumps up from his chair and shouts in the general direction of the orchestra.*

IVANOV: All right, all right!

(*The music cuts out. The* DOCTOR *pauses looking at* IVANOV.)

IVANOV: (*To the* DOCTOR) I'm sorry about that.

(IVANOV *sits down.*

*The* DOCTOR *sits down and all the strings accompany this movement into his chair.*

IVANOV *leaps up again.*)

(*Shouts.*) I'll have your gut for garters!

DOCTOR: Sit down, please.

IVANOV: (*Sitting down*) It's the only kind of language they understand.

DOCTOR: Did the pills help at all?

IVANOV: I don't know. What pills did you give them?

DOCTOR: Now look, *there is no orchestra*. We cannot make progress until we agree that there is no orchestra.

IVANOV: Or until we agree that there is.

DOCTOR: (*Slapping his violin, which is on the table*) But there is no orchestra.

(IVANOV *glances at the violin.*)

I have an orchestra, but you do not.

IVANOV: Does that seem reasonable to you?

DOCTOR: It just happens to be so. I play in an orchestra occasionally. It is my hobby. It is a real orchestra. Yours is not. I am a doctor. You are a patient. If I tell you you do not have an orchestra, it follows that you do not have an orchestra. If you tell me you have an orchestra, it follows that you do not have an orchestra. Or rather it does not follow that you do have an orchestra.

IVANOV: I am perfectly happy not to have an orchestra.

DOCTOR: Good.

IVANOV: I never asked to have an orchestra.

DOCTOR: Keep saying to yourself, 'I have no orchestra. I have never had an orchestra. I do not want an orchestra.'

IVANOV: Absolutely.

DOCTOR: 'There is no orchestra.'

IVANOV: All right.

DOCTOR: Good.

IVANOV: There is one thing you can do for me.

DOCTOR: Yes?

IVANOV: Stop them playing.

DOCTOR: They will stop playing when you understand that they
do not exist.

(IVANOV *gets up*.)

IVANOV: I have no orchestra.

(*Music. 1 chord.*)

I have never had an orchestra.

(*Music. 2 chords.*)

I do not want an orchestra.

(*Music. 3 chords.*)

There is no orchestra.

(*The orchestra takes off in triumph.*

*Light fades on* OFFICE, *comes up on* CELL.)


CELL

ALEXANDER *has been asleep on his bed the whole time.* IVANOV *returns
to the* CELL. *He picks up his triangle rod. He stands by* ALEXANDER'*s
bed looking down on him. The music continues and becomes threatening. It becomes nightmare music.* ALEXANDER'*s nightmare. The music
seems to be approaching violent catharsis. But* ALEXANDER *jumps
awake and the music cuts out in mid-bar.*

*Silence.*

IVANOV: Sorry. I can't control them.

ALEXANDER: Please . . .

IVANOV: Don't worry, I know how to handle myself. Any
trumpeter comes at me, I'll kick his teeth in. Violins get it
under the chin to boot, this boot, and God help anyone
who plays a cello. Do you play a musical instrument?

ALEXANDER: No.

IVANOV: Then you've got nothing to worry about. Tell me about
yourself—your home, your childhood, your first piano-
teacher . . . how did it all begin?

(*The next speech should be lit as a sort of solo. Musical annotation.*)

ALEXANDER: One day they arrested a friend of mine for possessing a controversial book, and they kept him in mental hospitals for a year and a half. I thought this was an odd thing to do. Soon after he got out, they arrested a couple of writers, A and B, who had published some stories abroad under different names. Under their own names they got five years' and seven years' hard labour. I thought this was most peculiar. My friend, C, demonstrated against the arrest of A and B. I told him he was crazy to do it, and they put him back into the mental hospital. D was a man who wrote to various people about the trial of A and B and held meetings with his friends E, F, G and H, who were all arrested, so I, J, K, L and a fifth man demonstrated against the arrest of E, F, G and H, and were themselves arrested. D was arrested the next day. The fifth man was my friend C, who had just got out of the mental hospital where they put him for demonstrating against the arrest of A and B, and I told him he was crazy to demonstrate against the arrest of E, F, G and H, and he got three years in a labour camp. I thought this really wasn't fair. M compiled a book on the trials of C, I, J, K and L, and with his colleagues N, O, P, Q, R and S attended the trial of T who had written a book about his experiences in a labour camp, and who got a year in a labour camp. In the courtroom it was learned that the Russian army had gone to the aid of Czechoslovakia. M, N, O, P, Q, R and S decided to demonstrate in Red Square the following Sunday, when they were all arrested and variously disposed of in labour camps, psychiatric hospitals and internal exile. Three years had passed since the arrest of A and B. C finished his sentence about the same time as A, and then he did something really crazy. He started telling everybody that sane people were being put in mental hospitals for their political opinions. By the time B finished his sentence, C was on trial for anti-Soviet agitation and slander, and he got seven years in prison and labour camps, and five years' exile.

You see all the trouble writers cause.

(*The children's percussion band re-enters as a discreet subtext.*)

They spoil things for ordinary people.

My childhood was uneventful. My adolescence was normal.
I got an ordinary job, and married a conventional girl who
died uncontroversially in childbirth. Until the child was
seven the only faintly interesting thing about me was that I
had a friend who kept getting arrested.

Then one day I did something really crazy.

(*The percussion is sabotaged exactly as before but this time by a
snare drum being violently beaten. It stops suddenly and the
light comes up on* SACHA *sitting at the desk with a punctured
drum on the desk, the* TEACHER *standing motionless in her position.
Optional: On tape the sound of a children's playground at
some distance.*)

SCHOOL

TEACHER: So this is how I am repaid. Is this how it began with
your father? First he smashes school property. Later he
keeps bad company. Finally, slanderous letters. Lies. To his
superiors. To the Party. To the newspapers. . . . To
foreigners. . . .

SACHA: Papa doesn't lie. He beat me when I did it.

TEACHER: *Lies!* Bombarding *Pravda* with lies! What did he
expect?

(*The light on the* TEACHER *and* SACHA *fades just after the
beginning of* ALEXANDER's *speech.*)

CELL

ALEXANDER: They put me in the Leningrad Special Psychiatric
Hospital on Arsenal'naya Street, where I was kept for thirty
months, including two months on hunger strike.

They don't like you to die unless you can die anonymously.
If your name is known in the West, it is an embarrassment.
The bad old days were over long ago. Things are different
now. Russia is a civilized country, very good at Swan Lake
and space technology, and it is confusing if people starve
themselves to death.

So after a couple of weeks they brought my son to persuade
me to eat. But although by this time he was nine years old
he was uncertain what to say.

(SACHA *speaks from the* SCHOOL, *not directly to* ALEXANDER.)

SACHA: I got a letter from abroad, with our picture in the newspaper.

ALEXANDER: What did it say?

SACHA: I don't know. It was all in English.

ALEXANDER: How is school?

SACHA: All right. I've started geometry. It's horrible.

ALEXANDER: How is Babushka?

SACHA: All right. You smell like Olga when she does her nails.

ALEXANDER: Who is Olga?

SACHA: She has your room now. Till you come back.

ALEXANDER: Good.

SACHA: Do they make you paint your nails here?

*(End of duologue. Return to solo.)*

ALEXANDER: If you don't eat for a long time you start to smell of acetone, which is the stuff girls use for taking the paint off their finger-nails. When the body runs out of protein and carbohydrate it starts to metabolize its own fat, and acetone is the waste product. To put this another way, a girl removing her nail-varnish smells of starvation.

After two months you could have removed nail-varnish with my urine, so they brought Sacha back, but when he saw me he couldn't speak—

SACHA: *(Cries)* Papa!

ALEXANDER: —and then they gave in. And when I was well enough they brought me here.

This means they have decided to let me go. It is much harder to get from Arsenal'naya to a civil hospital than from a civil hospital to the street. But it has to be done right. They don't want to lose ground. They need a formula. It will take a little time but that's all right. I shall read *War and Peace*.

Everything is going to be all right.

*(Orchestra.)*


SCHOOL

*This scene is enclosed inside music which ends up as the DOCTOR's violin solo into the following scene.*

SACHA: A triangle is the shortest distance between three points.

TEACHER: Rubbish.

SACHA: A circle is the longest distance to the same point.

TEACHER: Sacha!

SACHA: A plane area bordered by high walls is a prison not a hospital.

TEACHER: Be quiet!

SACHA: I don't care!—he was never sick at home. Never!

(*Music.*)

TEACHER: Stop crying.

(*Music.*)

Everything is going to be all right.

(*Music to violin solo.*

*Lights fade on* SCHOOL.)

OFFICE

DOCTOR *in his* OFFICE *playing violin solo. Violin cuts out.*

DOCTOR: Come in.

(ALEXANDER *enters the* DOCTOR'S *light.*)

DOCTOR: Hello. Sit down please. Do you play a musical instrument?

ALEXANDER: (*Taken aback*) Are you a patient?

DOCTOR: (*Cheerfully*) No, I am a doctor. *You* are a patient. It's a distinction which we try to keep going here, though I'm told it's coming under scrutiny in more advanced circles of psychiatric medicine. (*He carefully puts his violin into its case.*) (*Sententiously*) Yes, if everybody in the world played a violin, I'd be out of a job.

ALEXANDER: As a psychiatrist?

DOCTOR: No, as a violinist. The psychiatric hospitals would be packed to the doors. You obviously don't know much about musicians. Welcome to the Third Civil Mental Hospital. What can I do for you?

ALEXANDER: I have a complaint.

DOCTOR: (*Opening file*) Yes, I know—pathological development of the personality with paranoid delusions.

ALEXANDER: No, there's nothing the matter with me.

DOCTOR: (*Closing file*) There you are, you see.

ALEXANDER: My complaint is about the man in my cell.

DOCTOR: Ward.

ALEXANDER: He thinks he has an orchestra.

DOCTOR: Yes, he has an identity problem. I forget his name.

ALEXANDER: His behaviour is aggressive.

DOCTOR: He complains about you, too. Apparently you cough during the diminuendos.

ALEXANDER: Is there anything you can do?

DOCTOR: Certainly. (*Producing a red pill box from the drawer.*) Suck one of these every four hours.

ALEXANDER: But he's a raving lunatic.

DOCTOR: Of course. The idea that all the people locked up in mental hospitals are sane while the people walking about outside are all mad is merely a literary conceit, put about by people who should be locked up. I assure you there's not much in it. Taken as a whole, the sane are out there and the sick are in here. For example, *you* are here because you have delusions, that sane people are put in mental hospitals.

ALEXANDER: But I *am* in a mental hospital.

DOCTOR: That's what I said. If you're not prepared to discuss your case rationally, we're going to go round in circles. Did you say you *didn't* play a musical instrument, by the way?

ALEXANDER: No. Could I be put in a cell on my own?

DOCTOR: Look, let's get this clear. This is what is called an *Ordinary* Psychiatric Hospital, that is to say a civil mental hospital coming under the Ministry of Heath, and we have *wards*. Cells is what they have in prisons, and also, possibly, in what are called *Special* Psychiatric Hospitals, which come under the Ministry of Internal Affairs and are for prisoners who represent a special danger to society. Or rather, patients. No, you didn't say, or no you don't play one?

ALEXANDER: Could I be put in a ward on my own?

DOCTOR: I'm afraid not. Colonel—or rather Doctor—Rozinsky, who has taken over your case, chose your cell- or rather ward-mate personally.

ALEXANDER: He might kill me.

DOCTOR: We have to assume that Rozinsky knows what's best for you; though in my opinion you need a psychiatrist.

ALEXANDER: You mean he's not really a doctor?

DOCTOR: Of course he's a doctor and he is proud to serve the State in any capacity, but he was not actually trained in psychiatry *as such*.

ALEXANDER: What is his speciality?

DOCTOR: Semantics. He's a Doctor of Philology, whatever that means. I'm told he's a genius.

ALEXANDER: (*Angrily*) I won't see him.

DOCTOR: It may not be necessary. It seems to me that the best answer is for you to go home. Would Thursday suit you?

ALEXANDER: Thursday?

DOCTOR: Why not? There is an Examining Commission on Wednesday. We shall aim at curing your schizophrenia by Tuesday night, if possible by seven o'clock because I have a concert. (*He produces a large blue pill box.*) Take one of these every four hours.

ALEXANDER: What are they?

DOCTOR: A mild laxative.

ALEXANDER: For schizophrenia?

DOCTOR: The layman often doesn't realize that medicine advances in a series of imaginative leaps.

ALEXANDER: I see. Well, I suppose I'll have to read *War and Peace* some other time.

DOCTOR: Yes. Incidentally, when you go before the Commission try not to make any remark which might confuse them. I shouldn't mention *War and Peace* unless they mention it first. The sort of thing I'd stick to is 'Yes', if they ask you whether you agree you were mad; 'No', if they ask you whether you intend to persist in your slanders; 'Definitely', if they ask you whether your treatment has been satisfactory, and 'Sorry', if they ask you how you feel about it all, or if you didn't catch the question.

ALEXANDER: I was never mad, and my treatment was barbaric.

DOCTOR: Stupidity is one thing I can't cure. I have to show that I have treated you. You have to recant and show gratitude for the treatment. We have to act together.

ALEXANDER: The KGB broke my door and frightened my son and my mother-in-law. My madness consisted of writing to various people about a friend of mine who is in prison. This friend was twice put in mental hospitals for political reasons, and then they arrested him for saying that sane people were put in mental hospitals, and then they put him in prison because he was sane when he said this; and I said so, and

114

they put me in a mental hospital. And you are quite right—
in the Arsenal'naya they have cells. There are bars on the
windows, peepholes in the doors, and the lights burn all
night. It is run just like a gaol, with warders and trusties,
but the regime is more strict, and the male nurses are
convicted criminals serving terms for theft and violent
crimes, and they beat and humiliate the patients and steal
their food, and are protected by the doctors, some of whom
wear KGB uniforms under their white coats. For the
politicals, punishment and medical treatment are intimately
related. I was given injections of aminazin, sulfazin, triftazin,
haloperidol and insulin, which caused swellings, cramps,
headaches, trembling, fever and the loss of various abilities
including the ability to read, write, sleep, sit, stand, and
button my trousers. When all this failed to improve my
condition, I was stripped and bound head to foot with
lengths of wet canvas. As the canvas dried it became tighter
and tighter until I lost consciousness. They did this to me
for ten days in a row, and still my condition did not
improve.

Then I went on hunger strike. And when they saw I
intended to die they lost their nerve. And now you think
I'm going to crawl out of here, thanking them for curing
me of my delusions? Oh no. They lost. And they will have
to see that it is so. They have forgotten their mortality.
Losing might be their first touch of it for a long time.

(DOCTOR *picks up his violin.*)

DOCTOR: What about your son? He is turning into a delinquent.

(DOCTOR *plucks the violin EGBDF.*)

He's a good boy. He deserves a father.

(DOCTOR *plucks the violin . . .*)


SCHOOL

TEACHER: Things have changed since the bad old days. When I
was a girl there were terrible excesses. A man accused like
your father might well have been blameless. Now things are
different. The Constitution guarantees freedom of conscience,
freedom of the press, freedom of speech, of assembly, of
worship, and many other freedoms. The Soviet Constitution

has always been the most liberal in the world, ever since the
first Constitution was written after the Revolution.

SACHA: Who wrote it?

TEACHER: (*Hesitates*) His name was Nikolai Bukharin.

SACHA: Can we ask Nikolai Bukharin about papa?

TEACHER: Unfortunately he was shot soon after he wrote the
Constitution. Everything was different in those days.
Terrible things happened.


CELL

ALEXANDER *has just started to read 'War and Peace' and* IVANOV
*looks over his shoulder.*

IVANOV: 'Well, prince, Genoa and Lucca are no more than the
private estates of the Bonaparte family.'

(ALEXANDER *is nervous, and* IVANOV *becomes hysterical but still
reading.*)

'If you dare deny that this means war—'

(ALEXANDER *jumps up slamming the book shut and the orchestra
jumps into a few bars of the '1812'.* IVANOV *holds* ALEXANDER
*by the shoulders and there is a moment of suspense and
imminent violence, then* IVANOV *kisses* ALEXANDER *on both
cheeks.*)

Courage, mon brave!

Every member of the orchestra carries a baton in his
knapsack! Your turn will come.


OFFICE

DOCTOR: Next!

(ALEXANDER *goes into the* OFFICE.)

Your behaviour is causing alarm. I'm beginning to think
you're off your head. Quite apart from being a paranoid
schizophrenic. I have to consider seriously whether an
Ordinary Hospital can deal with your symptoms.

ALEXANDER: I have no symptoms, I have opinions.

DOCTOR: Your opinions are your symptoms. Your disease is
dissent. Your kind of schizophrenia does not presuppose
changes of personality noticeable to others. I might compare
your case to that of Pyotr Grigorenko of whom it has been
stated by our leading psychiatrists at the Serbsky Institute,

that his outwardly well adjusted behaviour and formally coherent utterances were indicative of a pathological development of the personality. Are you getting the message? I can't help you. And furthermore your breath stinks of aeroplane glue or something—what have you been eating?

ALEXANDER: Nothing.

DOCTOR: And that's something else—we have never had a hunger strike here, except once and that was in protest against the food, which is psychologically coherent and it did wonders for the patients' morale, though not for the food. . . .
(*Pause.*)
You can choose your own drugs.
You don't even have to take them.
Just say you took them.
(*Pause.*)
Well, what do you *want*?

ALEXANDER: (*Flatly, not poetically*)
> I want to get back to the bad old times
> when a man got a sentence appropriate to his crimes—
> ten years' hard for a word out of place,
> twenty-five years if they didn't like your face,
> and no one pretended that you were off your head.
> In the good old Archipelago you're either well or
>     dead—
> And the—

DOCTOR: Stop it!
My God, how long can you go on like that?

ALEXANDER: In the Arsenal'naya I was not allowed writing materials, on medical grounds. If you want to remember things it helps if they rhyme.

DOCTOR: You gave me a dreadful shock. I thought I had discovered an entirely new form of mental disturbance.
Immortality smiled upon me, one quick smile, and was gone.

ALEXANDER: Your name may not be entirely lost to history.

DOCTOR: What do you mean?—it's not *me*! I'm told what to do.
Look, if you'll eat something I'll send for your son.

ALEXANDER: I don't want him to come here.

DOCTOR: If you don't eat something I'll send for your son.
(*Pause.*)

You mustn't be so rigid.

(ALEXANDER *starts to leave.*

*Pause.*)

Did the pills help at all?

ALEXANDER: I don't know.

DOCTOR: Do you believe that sane people are put in mental hospitals?

ALEXANDER: Yes.

DOCTOR: They didn't help.

ALEXANDER: I gave them to Ivanov. *His* name is also Ivanov.

DOCTOR: So it is. That's why Colonel or rather Doctor Rozinsky insisted you shared his cell, or rather ward.

ALEXANDER: Because we have the same name?

DOCTOR: The man is a genius. The layman often doesn't realize that medicine advances in—

ALEXANDER: I know. I have been giving Ivanov my rations. He needed a laxative. I gave him my pills.

(ALEXANDER *leaves.*)

DOCTOR: Next!

(IVANOV *enters immediately, with his triangle, almost crossing* ALEXANDER.

IVANOV *is transformed, triumphant, awe-struck.*)

Hello, Ivanov. Did the pills help at all?

(IVANOV *strikes his triangle.*)

IVANOV: I have no orchestra!

(*Silence.*)

IVANOV *indicates the silence with a raised finger. He strikes his triangle again.*)

DOCTOR: (*Suddenly*) Wait a minute!—what day is it?

IVANOV: I have never *had* an orchestra!

(*Silence.*

*The* DOCTOR, *however, has become preoccupied and misses the significance of this.*)

DOCTOR: *What day is it?* Tuesday?

(IVANOV *strikes the triangle.*)

IVANOV: I do not want an orchestra!

(*Silence.*)

DOCTOR: (*Horrified*) What time is it? I'm going to be late for the orchestra!

*(The* DOCTOR *grabs his violin case and starts to leave.* IVANOV *strikes his triangle.)*

IVANOV: *There is no orchestra!*

DOCTOR: *(Leaving)* Of course there's a bloody orchestra!

*(Music—one chord.* IVANOV *hears it and is mortified. More chords. The* DOCTOR *has left.)*

IVANOV: *(Bewildered)* I have an orchestra.

*(Music.)*

I've *always* had an orchestra.

*(Music.)*

I always *knew* I had an orchestra.

*(Music.*

ALEXANDER *has gone to sit on his bed.* IVANOV *sits in the* DOCTOR's *chair. The* DOCTOR *joins the violinists.* SACHA *moves across towards* IVANOV.

*The music continues and ends.)*

IVANOV: Come in.

SACHA: Alexander Ivanov, sir.

IVANOV: Absolutely correct. Who are you?

SACHA: Alexander Ivanov, sir.

IVANOV: The boy's a fool.

SACHA: They said to come, sir. Is it about my father?

IVANOV: What's his name?

SACHA: Alexander Ivanov, sir.

IVANOV: This place is a madhouse.

SACHA: I know, sir.

Are you the doctor?

IVANOV: *Ivanov!* Of course. Sad case.

SACHA: What's the matter with him?

IVANOV: Tone deaf. Are you musical at all?

SACHA: No, sir.

IVANOV: What is your instrument?

SACHA: Triangle, sir.

Is it about *that* that I'm here?

IVANOV: Certainly, what else?

SACHA: Drum, sir.

IVANOV: What?

SACHA: Don't make me stay! I'll go back in the orchestra!

IVANOV: You can be in mine.

SACHA: I can't play anything, really.

IVANOV: Everyone is equal to the triangle. That is the first axiom of Euclid, the Greek musician.

SACHA: Yes, sir.

IVANOV: The second axiom! It is easier for a sick man to play the triangle than for a camel to play the triangle.

The third axiom!—even a camel can play the triangle!

The *pons asinorum* of Euclid! Anyone can play the triangle no matter how sick!

SACHA: Yes, sir—(*Crying.*)—please will you put me with Papa?

IVANOV (*Raving*) The five postulates of Euclid!

A triangle with a bass is a combo!

Two triangles sharing the same bass is a trio!

SACHA: Are you the doctor?

IVANOV: A trombone is the longest distance between two points!

SACHA: You're not the doctor.

IVANOV: A string has length but no point.

SACHA: (*Cries*) Papa!

IVANOV: What is the Golden Rule?

SACHA: Papa!

IVANOV: (*Shouts*) A line *must be drawn*!

SACHA *runs out of* IVANOV's *light and moves into the orchestra among the players. The next four of* SACHA's *speeches, which are sung, come from different positions as he moves around the orchestra platform. There is music involved in the following scene.*

SACHA: (*Sings*) Papa, where've they put you?

    (ALEXANDER's '*poems*' *are uttered rapidly on a single rhythm.*)

ALEXANDER: Dear Sacha, don't be sad,

        it would have been ten times as bad

        if we hadn't had the time we had,

        so think of that and please be glad.

        I kiss you now, your loving dad.

        Don't let them tell you I was mad.

SACHA: (*Sings*) Papa, don't be rigid!

    Everything can be all right!

ALEXANDER: Dear Sacha, try to see

        what they call their liberty

        is just the freedom to agree

that one and one is sometimes three.
I kiss you now, remember me.
Don't neglect your geometry.

SACHA: (*Sings*) Papa, don't be rigid!
Everything can be all right!

ALEXANDER: Dear Sacha, when I'd dead,
I'll be living in your head,
which is what your mama said,
keep her picture by your bed.
I kiss you now, and don't forget,
if you're brave the best is yet.

SACHA: (*Sings*) Papa, don't be rigid!
Be brave and tell them lies!

CELL

SACHA: (*Not singing*) Tell them lies. Tell them they've cured you.
Tell them you're grateful.

ALEXANDER: How can that be right?

SACHA: If they're wicked how can it be wrong?

ALEXANDER: It helps them to go on being wicked. It helps people
to think that perhaps they're not so wicked after all.

SACHA: It doesn't matter. I want you to come home.

ALEXANDER: And what about all the other fathers? And mothers?

SACHA: (*Shouts*) It's wicked to let yourself die!

(SACHA *leaves*.)


*The* DOCTOR *moves from the orchestra to the* SCHOOL.

DOCTOR: Ivanov!

ALEXANDER: Dear Sacha—
be glad of—
kiss Mama's picture—
good-bye.

DOCTOR: Ivanov!

(IVANOV *moves to* CELL.)

Ivanov!

(SACHA *moves towards the* SCHOOL.)

ALEXANDER: (*Rapidly as before*)
Dear Sacha, I love you,
I hope you love me too.

121

To thine own self be true
one and one is always two.
I kiss you now, adieu.
There was nothing else to do.


SCHOOL

SACHA *arrives at* SCHOOL. DOCTOR *is there.*

TEACHER *has remained near the desk.*

TEACHER: Sacha. Did you persuade him?

SACHA: He's going to die.

DOCTOR: I'm not allowed to let him die.

SACHA: Then let him go.

DOCTOR: I'm not allowed to let him go till he admits he's cured.

SACHA: Then he'll die.

DOCTOR: He'd rather die than admit he's cured? This is madness,
and it's not allowed!

SACHA: Then you'll have to let him go.

DOCTOR: I'm not allowed to—it's a logical impasse. Did you tell
him he mustn't be so rigid?

SACHA: If you want to get rid of Papa, *you* must not be rigid!

DOCTOR: What shall I tell the Colonel? He's a genius but he
can't do the impossible.

(*Organ music. The* COLONEL's *entrance is as impressive as
possible. The organ accompanies his entrance.*

*The* DOCTOR *moves to meet him. The* COLONEL *ignores the*
DOCTOR. *He stops in front of* ALEXANDER *and* IVANOV. *When
the organ music stops the* COLONEL *speaks.*)


CELL

COLONEL: Ivanov!

(ALEXANDER *and* IVANOV *stand up.*)

(*To* IVANOV.) Alexander Ivanov?

IVANOV: Yes.

COLONEL: Do you believe that sane people are put in mental
hospitals?

DOCTOR: Excuse me, Doctor—

COLONEL: Shut up!—

(*To* IVANOV.) Well? Would a Soviet doctor put a sane man
into a lunatic asylum, in your opinion?

122

IVANOV: (*Baffled*) I shouldn't think so. Why?

COLONEL: (*Briskly*) Quite right! How do you feel?

IVANOV: Fit as a fiddle, thank you.

COLONEL: Quite right!

(*The* COLONEL *turns to* ALEXANDER.)

Alexander Ivanov?

ALEXANDER: Yes.

COLONEL: Do you have an orchestra?

(IVANOV *opens his mouth to speak.*)

(*To* IVANOV.) Shut up!

(*To* ALEXANDER.) Well?

ALEXANDER: No.

COLONEL: Do you hear any music of any kind?

ALEXANDER: No.

COLONEL: How do you feel?

ALEXANDER: All right.

COLONEL: Manners!

ALEXANDER: Thank you.

COLONEL: (*To* DOCTOR) There's absolutely nothing wrong with these men. Get them out of here.

DOCTOR: Yes, Colonel—Doctor.

(*The* COLONEL's *exit is almost as impressive as his entrance, also with organ music. But this time the organ music blends into orchestral music—the finale.*)

*The* TEACHER *moves into the orchestra. The* DOCTOR *moves to the violins taking his instrument and joining in.* IVANOV *takes his triangle and joins the percussionists and beats the triangle.*

SACHA *comes across to the middle of the platform at the bottom. These directions assume a centre aisle going up the middle of the orchestra towards the organ.* ALEXANDER *and* SACHA *move up this aisle,* SACHA *running ahead. At the top he turns and sings to the same tune as before:*

SACHA: (*Sings*) Papa, don't be crazy!

Everything can be all right!

ALEXANDER: Sacha—

SACHA: (*Sings*) Everything can be all right!

(*Music. Music ends.*)

123

# PROFESSIONAL FOUL

A Play for Television

To Vaclav Havel

## Characters

ANDERSON
MCKENDRICK
CHETWYN
HOLLAR
BROADBENT
CRISP
STONE
CAPTAIN (MAN 6)
POLICEMAN (MAN 1)
POLICEMAN (MAN 2)
POLICEMAN (MAN 3)
POLICEMAN (MAN 4)
POLICEMAN (MAN 5)
MRS HOLLAR
SACHA (ten years old)
GRAYSON
CHAMBERLAIN
FRENCHMAN
CHAIRMAN
CLERK, LIFT OPERATORS, CONCIERGES,
INTERPRETERS, CUSTOMS, POLICE, etc.

*Professional Foul* was first shown on BBC TV in September 1977. The cast was as follows:

| | |
|---|---|
| ANDERSON | Peter Barkworth |
| MCKENDRICK | John Shrapnel |
| CHETWYN | Richard O'Callaghan |
| HOLLAR | Stephen Rea |
| BROADBENT | Bernard Hill |
| CRISP | Billy Hamon |
| STONE | Shane Rimmer |
| CAPTAIN | David de Keyser |
| MAN 1 | Ludwig Lang |
| MAN 2 | Milos Kirek |
| MAN 3 | Arnoft Kopecky |
| MAN 4 | Paul Moritz |
| MRS HOLLAR | Susan Strawson |
| SACHA | Stefan Ceba |
| GRAYSON | Sam Kelly |
| CHAMBERLAIN | Victor Longley |
| FRENCHMAN | Graeme Eton |
| CHAIRMAN | Ivan Jelinek |
| CLERK | Patrick Monckton |
| INTERPRETER | Sandra Frieze |
| | |
| Script Editor | Richard Broke |
| Designer | Don Taylor |
| Producer | Mark Shivas |
| Director | Michael Lindsay-Hogg |

1. INT. AEROPLANE. IN FLIGHT

*The tourist class cabin of a passenger jet.*

*We are mainly concerned with two passengers.* ANDERSON *is an Ox-bridge don, a professor. He is middle-aged, or more. He is sitting in an aisle seat, on the left as we look down the gangway towards the tail.* MCKENDRICK *is also in an aisle seat, but across the gangway and one row nearer the tail.* MCKENDRICK *is about forty. He is also a don, but where* ANDERSON *gives a somewhat fastidious impression,* MCKENDRICK *is a rougher sort of diamond.*

MCKENDRICK *is sitting in the first row of smokers' seats, and* ANDERSON *in the last row of the non-smokers' seats looking aft.*

*The plane is by no means full. The three seats across the aisle from* ANDERSON *are vacant. The seat next to* ANDERSON *on his right is also vacant but the seat beyond that, by the window, accommodates a* SLEEPING MAN.

*On the vacant seat between* ANDERSON *and the* SLEEPING MAN *is lying a sex magazine of the* Penthouse *type. The magazine, however, is as yet face down.*

*The passengers are coming to the end of a meal. They have trays of aeroplane food in front of them.*

MCKENDRICK *puts down his fork and lights a cigarette.*

ANDERSON *dabs at his mouth with his napkin and puts it down. He glances around casually and notes the magazine next to him. He notes the* SLEEPING MAN.

MCKENDRICK *has a briefcase on the seat next to him, and from this he takes a glossy brochure. In fact, this is quite an elaborate publication associated with a philosophical congress. The cover of this programme is seen to read: 'Colloquium Philosophicum Prague 77'.*

ANDERSON *slides out from under his lunch tray a brochure identical to* MCKENDRICK'S. *He glances at it for a mere moment and loses interest. He turns his attention back to the magazine on the seat. He turns the*

*magazine over and notes the naked woman on its cover. He picks the*
*magazine up, with a further glance at the* SLEEPING MAN, *and opens*
*it to a spread of colour photographs. Consciously or unconsciously he*
*is holding the brochure in such a way as to provide a shield for the*
*magazine.*

MCKENDRICK *casually glancing round, sees the twin to his own*
*brochure.*


MCKENDRICK: Snap.

> (ANDERSON *looks up guiltily.*)

ANDERSON: Ah . . .

> (ANDERSON *closes the magazine and slides it face-up under his*
> *lunch tray.*
> MCKENDRICK'S *manner is extrovert. Almost breezy.*
> ANDERSON'S *manner is a little vague.*)

MCKENDRICK: I wasn't sure it was you. Not a very good likeness.

ANDERSON: I assure you this is how I look.

MCKENDRICK: I mean your photograph. (*He flips his brochure*
> *open. It contains small photographs and pen portraits of various*
> *men and women who are in fact to be speakers at the colloquium.*)
> The photograph is younger.

ANDERSON: It must be an old photograph.

> (MCKENDRICK *gets up and comes to sit in the empty seat across*
> *the aisle from* ANDERSON.)

MCKENDRICK: (*Changing seats*) Bill McKendrick.

ANDERSON: How odd.

MCKENDRICK: Is it?

ANDERSON: Young therefore old. Old therefore young. Only odd
> at first glance.

MCKENDRICK: Oh yes.

> (ANDERSON *takes a notebook, with pencil attached, from his*
> *pocket and writes in it as he speaks.*)

ANDERSON: The second glance is known as linguistic analysis. A
> lot of chaps pointing out that we don't always mean what
> we say, even when we manage to say what we mean.
> Personally I'm quite prepared to believe it. (*He finishes*
> *writing and closes the notebook. He glances uneasily out of the*
> *window.*) Have you noticed the way the wings keep *wagging*?
> I try to look away and think of something else but I am

130

drawn back irresistibly . . . I wouldn't be nervous about
flying if the wings didn't wag. Solid steel. Thick as a bank
safe. Flexing like tree branches. It's not natural. There is a
coldness around my heart as though I'd seen your
cigarette smoke knock against the ceiling and break in two
like a bread stick. By the way, that is a non-smoking seat.

MCKENDRICK: Sorry

(MCKENDRICK *stubs out his cigarette.* ANDERSON *puts his notebook
back into his pocket.*)

ANDERSON: Yes, I like to collect little curiosities for the language
chaps. It's like handing round a bag of liquorice allsorts.
They're terribly grateful. (*A thought strikes him.*) Oh, you're
not a language chap yourself?

(*The question seems to surprise* MCKENDRICK, *and amuse him.*)

MCKENDRICK: No. I'm McKendrick.

ANDERSON: You'll be giving a paper?

MCKENDRICK: Yes. Nothing new, actually. More of a summing-up
of my corner. My usual thing, you know . . . ?

(MCKENDRICK *is fishing but* ANDERSON *doesn't seem to notice.*)

ANDERSON: Jolly good.

MCKENDRICK: Perhaps you've come across some of my stuff . . . ?

(ANDERSON *now wakes up to the situation and is contrite.*)

ANDERSON: Clearly that is a reasonable expectation. I *am* sorry.
I'm sure I know your name. I don't read the philosophical
journals as much as I should, and hardly ever go to these
international bunfights. No time nowadays. They shouldn't
call us professors. It's more like being the faculty almoner.

MCKENDRICK: At least my paper will be new to you. We are the
only English, actually singing for our supper, I mean. I
expect there'll be a few others going for the free trip and
the social life. In fact, I see we've got one on board. At the
back.

(MCKENDRICK *jerks his head towards the back of the plane.*
ANDERSON *turns round to look. The object of attention is*
CHETWYN, *asleep in the back row, on the aisle.* CHETWYN *is
younger than* MCKENDRICK *and altogether frailer and neater.*
ANDERSON *squints down the plane at* CHETWYN.)

Do you know Prague?

ANDERSON: (*Warily*) Not personally. I know the name. (*Then he wakes up to that*.) Oh, *Prague*. Sorry. No, I've never been there. (*Small pause*.) Or have I? I got an honorary degree at Bratislava once. We changed planes in Prague. (*Pause*.) It might have been Vienna actually. (*Pause. He looks at the window*.) Wag, wag.

MCKENDRICK: It's Andrew Chetwyn. Do you know him?

ANDERSON: (*Warily*) Not personally.

MCKENDRICK: I don't know him *personally*. Do you know his line at all?

ANDERSON: Not as such.

MCKENDRICK: (*Suspiciously*) Have you *heard* of him?

ANDERSON: No. In a word.

MCKENDRICK: Oh. He's been quite public recently.

ANDERSON: He's an ethics chap is he?

MCKENDRICK: His line is that Aristotle got it more or less right, and St Augustine brought it up to date.

ANDERSON: I can see that that might make him conspicuous.

MCKENDRICK: Oh, it's not *that*. I mean politics. Letters to *The Times* about persecuted professors with unpronounceable names. I'm surprised the Czechs gave him a visa.

ANDERSON: There are some rather dubious things happening in Czechoslovakia. Ethically.

MCKENDRICK: Oh yes. No doubt.

ANDERSON: We must not try to pretend otherwise.

MCKENDRICK: Oh quite. I mean I don't. My work is pretty political. I mean by implication, of course. As yours is. I'm looking forward to hearing you.

ANDERSON: Thank you. I'm sure your paper will be very interesting too.

MCKENDRICK: As a matter of fact I think there's a lot of juice left in the fictions problem.

ANDERSON: Is that what you're speaking on?

MCKENDRICK: No—you are.

ANDERSON: Oh, am I? (*He looks in his brochure briefly*.) So I am.

MCKENDRICK: 'Ethical Fictions as Ethical Foundations'.

ANDERSON: Yes. To tell you the truth I have an ulterior motive for coming to Czechoslovakia at this time. I'm being a tiny bit naughty.

MCKENDRICK: Naughty?

ANDERSON: Unethical. Well, I am being paid for by the Czech government, after all.

MCKENDRICK: And what . . . ?

ANDERSON: I don't think I'm going to tell you. You see, if I tell you I make you a co-conspirator whether or not you would have wished to be one. Ethically I should give you the opportunity of choosing to be one or not.

MCKENDRICK: Then why don't you give me the opportunity?

ANDERSON: I can't without telling you. An impasse.

(MCKENDRICK *is already putting two and two together and cannot hide his curiosity.*)

MCKENDRICK: Look . . . Professor Anderson . . . if it's political in any way I'd really be very interested.

ANDERSON: Why, are you a politics chap?

MCKENDRICK: One is naturally interested in what is happening in these places. And I have an academic interest—my field is the philosophical assumptions of social science.

ANDERSON: How fascinating. What is that exactly?

MCKENDRICK: (*Slightly hurt*) Perhaps my paper tomorrow afternoon will give you a fair idea.

ANDERSON: (*Mortified*) Tomorrow afternoon? I say, what rotten luck. That's exactly when I have to play truant. I *am* sorry.

MCKENDRICK: (*Coldly*) That's all right.

ANDERSON: I expect they'll have copies.

MCKENDRICK: I expect so.

ANDERSON: The science of social philosophy, eh?

MCKENDRICK: (*Brusquely*) More or less.

ANDERSON: (*With polite interest*) McCarthy.

MCKENDRICK: McKendrick.

ANDERSON: And how are things at . . . er . . .

MCKENDRICK: Stoke.

ANDERSON: (*Enthusiastically*) Stoke! An excellent university, I believe.

MCKENDRICK: You know perfectly well you wouldn't be seen dead in it.

(ANDERSON *considers this.*)

ANDERSON: Even if that were true, my being seen dead in a place has never so far as I know been thought a condition of its excellence.

(MCKENDRICK *despite himself laughs, though somewhat bitterly.*)

MCKENDRICK: Very good.

(*An* AIR HOSTESS *is walking down the aisle removing people's lunch trays. She removes* ANDERSON'*s tray, revealing the cover of the sexy magazine, in the middle of* MCKENDRICK'*s next speech and passes down the aisle.*)

Wit and paradox. Verbal felicity. An occupation for gentlemen. A higher civilization alive and well in the older universities. I see you like tits and bums, by the way.

ANDERSON: (*Embarrassed*) Ah . . .

(*The turning of tables cheers* MCKENDRICK *up considerably.*)

MCKENDRICK: They won't let you in with that you know. You'll have to hide it.

ANDERSON: As a matter of fact it doesn't belong to me.

MCKENDRICK: Western decadence you see. Marxists are a terrible lot of prudes. I can say that because I'm a bit that way myself.

ANDERSON: You surprise me.

MCKENDRICK: Mind you, when I say I'm a Marxist . . .

ANDERSON: Oh, I see.

MCKENDRICK: . . . I don't mean I'm an apologist for everything done in the name of Marxism.

ANDERSON: No, no quite. There's nothing anti-socialist about it. Quite the reverse. The rich have always had it to themselves.

MCKENDRICK: On the contrary. That's why I'd be really very interested in any extra-curricular activities which might be going. I have an open mind about it.

ANDERSON: (*His wires crossed*) Oh, yes, indeed, so have I.

MCKENDRICK: I sail pretty close to the wind, Marx-wise.

ANDERSON: Mind you, it's an odd thing but travel broadens the mind in a way that the proverbialist didn't quite intend. It's only at airports and railway stations that one finds in oneself a curiosity about er—er—erotica, um, girly magazines.

(MCKENDRICK *realizes that they've had their wires crossed.*)

MCKENDRICK: Perhaps you've come across some of my articles.

ANDERSON: (*Amazed and fascinated*) You mean you write for—? (*He pulls himself up and together.*) Oh—your—er articles— I'm afraid as I explained I'm not very good at keeping up with the philosophical. . . .

(MCKENDRICK *has gone back to his former seat to fish about in his briefcase. He emerges with another girly magazine and hands it along the aisle to* ANDERSON.)

MCKENDRICK: I've got one here. Page sixty-one. The Science Fiction short story. Not a bad life. Science Fiction and sex. And, of course, the philosophical assumptions of social science.

ANDERSON: (*Faintly*) Thank you very much.

MCKENDRICK: Keep it by all means.

(ANDERSON *cautiously thumbs through pages of naked women.*) I wonder if there'll be any decent women?

## 2. INT. HOTEL LOBBY. PRAGUE

*We are near the reception desk.* ANDERSON, MCKENDRICK *and* CHETWYN *have just arrived together. Perhaps with other people. Their luggage consists only of small overnight suitcases and briefcases.*

MCKENDRICK *is at the desk half-way through his negotiations. The lobby ought to be rather large, with lifts, etc. It should be large enough to make inconspicuous a* MAN *who is carefully watching the three Englishmen. This* MAN *is aged thirty-five or younger. He is poorly dressed, but not tramp-like. His name is* PAVEL HOLLAR. *The lobby contains other people and a poorly equipped news-stand.*

*We catch up with* ANDERSON *talking to* CHETWYN.

ANDERSON (*Enthusiastically*) Birmingham! Excellent university. Some very good people.

(*The desk* CLERK *comes to the counter where* MCKENDRICK *is first in the queue. The* CLERK *and other Czech people in this script obviously speak with an accent but there is no attempt here to reproduce it.*)

CLERK: Third floor. Dr McKendrick.

MCKENDRICK: Only of philosophy.

CLERK: Your baggage is there?

MCKENDRICK: (*Hastily*) Oh, I'll see to that. Can I have the key, please?

CLERK: Third floor. Dr Anderson. Ninth floor. A letter for you.

(*The* CLERK *gives* ANDERSON *a sealed envelope and also a key.* ANDERSON *seems to have been expecting the letter. He thanks the* CLERK *and takes it.*)

Dr Chetwyn ninth floor.

(*The three philosophers walk towards the lifts.* PAVEL *watches them go. When they reach the lift* ANDERSON *glances round and sees two men some way off across the lobby, perhaps at the news-stand. These men are called* CRISP *and* BROADBENT. CRISP *look very young, he is twenty-two. He wears a very smart, slightly flashy suit and tie.* BROADBENT *balding but young, in his thirties. He wears flannels and a blazer.* CRISP *is quite small.* BROADBENT *is big and heavy. But both look fit.*)

ANDERSON: I say, look who's over there . . . Broadbent and Crisp.

(*The lift now opens before them.* ANDERSON *goes in showing his key to the middle-aged* WOMAN *in charge of the lift.*
MCKENDRICK *and* CHETWYN *do likewise. Over this:*)

CHETWYN: Who? (*He sees them and recognizes them.*) Oh yes.

MCKENDRICK: (*Sees them.*) Who?

CHETWYN: Crisp and Broadbent. They must be staying here too.

MCKENDRICK: Crisp? Broadbent? That kid over by the news-stand?

ANDERSON: That's Crisp.

MCKENDRICK: My God, they get younger all the time.

(*The lift doors close.*
*Inside the lift.*)

ANDERSON: Crisp is twenty-two. Broadbent is past his peak but Crisp is the next genius in my opinion.

MCKENDRICK: Do you know him?

ANDERSON: Not personally. I've been watching him for a couple of years.

CHETWYN: He's Newcastle, isn't he?

ANDERSON: Yes.

MCKENDRICK: I've never heard of him. What's his role there?

ANDERSON: He's what used to be called left wing. Broadbent's in the centre. He's an opportunist more than anything.

(*The lift has stopped at the third floor.*)

(*To* MCKENDRICK.) This is you—see you later.

(MCKENDRICK *steps out of the lift and looks round.*)

MCKENDRICK: Do you think the rooms are bugged?

(*The lift doors shut him off.*
*Inside the lift.* ANDERSON *and* CHETWYN *ride up in silence for*

*a few moments.*)

ANDERSON: What was it Aristotle said about the higher you go
the further you fall . . . ?

CHETWYN: He was talking about tragic heroes.

(*The lift stops at the ninth floor.* ANDERSON *and* CHETWYN
*leave the lift.*)

I'm this way. There's a restaurant downstairs. The menu is
very limited but it's all right.

ANDERSON: You've been here before?

CHETWYN: Yes. Perhaps see you later then, sir.

(CHETWYN *goes down a corridor away from* ANDERSON'*s
corridor.*)

ANDERSON: (*To himself*) Sir?

(ANDERSON *follows the arrow towards his own room number.*)


3. INT. ANDERSON'S HOTEL ROOM

*The room contains a bed, a wardrobe, a chest. A telephone. A bath-
room containing a bath leads off through a door.*

ANDERSON *is unpacking. He puts some clothes into a drawer and closes
it. His suitcase is open on the bed.* ANDERSON *turns his attention to his
briefcase and brings out* MCKENDRICK'*s magazine. He looks round
wondering what to do with it. There is a knock on the door.* ANDERSON
*tosses the girly magazine into his suitcase and closes the case. He goes to
open the door. The caller is* PAVEL HOLLAR.

ANDERSON: Yes?

HOLLAR: I am Pavel Hollar.

ANDERSON: Yes?

HOLLAR: Professor Anderson.

(HOLLAR *is Czech and speaks with an accent.*)

ANDERSON: Hollar? Oh, heavens, yes. How extraordinary. Come
in.

HOLLAR: Thank you. I'm sorry to—

ANDERSON: No, no—what a pleasant surprise. I've only just
arrived as you can see. Sit where you can. How are you?
What are you doing? You live in Prague?

HOLLAR: Oh yes.

(ANDERSON *closes the door.*)

ANDERSON: Well, well. Well, well, well, well. How are you?
Must be ten years.

137

HOLLAR: Yes. It is ten. I took my degree in sixty-seven.

ANDERSON: You got a decent degree, too, didn't you?

HOLLAR: Yes, I got a first.

ANDERSON: Of course you did. Well done, well done. Are you still in philosophy?

HOLLAR: No, unfortunately.

ANDERSON: Ah. What are you doing now?

HOLLAR: I am a what do you say—a cleaner.

ANDERSON: (*With intelligent interest*) A cleaner? What is that?

HOLLAR: (*Surprised*) Cleaning. Washing. With a brush and a bucket. I am a cleaner at the bus station.

ANDERSON: You wash buses?

HOLLAR: No, not buses—the lavatories, the floors where people walk and so on.

ANDERSON: Oh. I see. You're a *cleaner*.

HOLLAR: Yes.

(*Pause.*)

ANDERSON: Are you married now, or anything?

HOLLAR: Yes. I married. She was almost my fiancée when I went to England. Irma. She is a country girl. No English. No philosophy. We have a son who is Sacha. That is Alexander.

ANDERSON: I see.

HOLLAR: And Mrs Anderson?

ANDERSON: She died. Did you meet her ever?

HOLLAR: No.

ANDERSON: (*Pause*) I don't know what to say.

HOLLAR: Did she die recently?

ANDERSON: No, I mean—a cleaner.

HOLLAR: I had one year graduate research. My doctorate studies were on certain connections with Thomas Paine and Locke. But then, since sixty-nine. . . .

ANDERSON: Cleaning lavatories.

HOLLAR: First I was in a bakery. Later on construction, building houses. Many other things. It is the way it is for many people.

ANDERSON: Is it all right for you to be here talking to me?

HOLLAR: Of course. Why not? You are my old professor.

(HOLLAR *is carrying a bag or briefcase. He puts this down and opens it.*)

I have something here.

(*From the bag he takes out the sort of envelope which would contain about thirty type-written foolscap pages. He also takes out a child's 'magic eraser' pad, the sort of pad on which one scratches a message and then slides it out to erase it.*)

You understand these things of course?

ANDERSON: (*Nonplussed*) Er . . .

HOLLAR: (*Smiling*) Of course.

(HOLLAR *demonstrates the pad briefly, then writes on the pad while Anderson watches.*)

ANDERSON: (*Stares at him*) To England?

(HOLLAR *abandons the use of the pad, and whispers in* ANDERSON's *ear.*)

HOLLAR: Excuse me.

(HOLLAR *goes to the door and opens it for* ANDERSON. HOLLAR *carries his envelope but leaves his bag in the room.* ANDERSON *goes out of the door baffled.* HOLLAR *follows him. They walk a few paces down the corridor.*)

Thank you. It is better to be careful.

ANDERSON: Why? You don't seriously suggest that my room is bugged?

HOLLAR: It is better to assume it.

ANDERSON: Why?

(*Just then the door of the room next to* ANDERSON's *opens and a* MAN *comes out. He is about forty and wears a dark rather shapeless suit. He glances at* ANDERSON *and* HOLLAR. *And then walks off in the opposite direction towards the lifts and passes out of sight.* HOLLAR *and* ANDERSON *instinctively pause until the* MAN *has gone.*)

I hope you're not getting me into trouble.

HOLLAR: I hope not. I don't think so. I have friends in trouble.

ANDERSON: I know, it's dreadful—but . . . well, what is it?

(HOLLAR *indicates his envelope.*)

HOLLAR: My doctoral thesis. It is mainly theoretical. Only ten thousand words, but very formally arranged.

ANDERSON: My goodness . . . ten years in the writing.

HOLLAR: No. I wrote it this month—when I heard of this congress here and you coming. I decided. Everyday in the night.

ANDERSON: Of course. I'd be very happy to read it.

HOLLAR: It is in Czech.

ANDERSON: Oh . . . well . . . ?

HOLLAR: I'm afraid so. But Peter Volkansky—he was with me,
you remember—we came together in sixty-three—

ANDERSON: Oh yes—Volkansky—yes, I do remember him. He
never came back here.

HOLLAR: No. He didn't come back. He was a realist.

ANDERSON: He's at Reading or somewhere like that.

HOLLAR: Lyster.

ANDERSON: Leicester. Exactly. Are you in touch with him?

HOLLAR: A little. He will translate it and try to have it published
in English. If it's good. I think it is good.

ANDERSON: But can't you publish it in Czech? . . . (*This catches
up on him and he shakes his head.*) Oh, Hollar . . . now, you
know, really, I'm a guest of the government here.

HOLLAR: They would not search you.

ANDERSON: That's not the point. I'm sorry . . . I mean it would
be bad manners, wouldn't it?

HOLLAR: Bad manners?

ANDERSON: I know it sounds rather lame. But ethics and manners
are interestingly related. The history of human calumny is
largely a series of breaches of good manners. . . . (*Pause.*)
Perhaps if I said correct behaviour it wouldn't sound so
ridiculous. You do see what I mean. I am sorry. . . . Look,
can we go back . . . I ought to unpack.

HOLLAR: My thesis is about correct behaviour.

ANDERSON: Oh yes?

HOLLAR: Here you know, individual correctness is defined by
what is correct for the State.

ANDERSON: Yes, I know.

HOLLAR: I ask how collective right can have meaning by itself.
I ask where it comes from, the idea of a collective ethic.

ANDERSON: Yes.

HOLLAR: I reply, it comes from the individual. One man's
dealings with another man.

ANDERSON: Yes.

HOLLAR: The collective ethic can only be the individual ethic
writ big.

ANDERSON: Writ large.

HOLLAR: Writ large, precisely. The ethics of the State must be judged against the fundamental ethic of the individual. The human being, not the citizen. I conclude there is an obligation, a human responsibility, to fight against the State correctness. Unfortunately that is not a safe conclusion.

ANDERSON: Quite. The difficulty arises when one asks oneself how the *individual* ethic can have any meaning by itself. Where does *that* come from? In what sense is it intelligible, for example, to say that a man has certain inherent, individual rights? It is much easier to understand how a community of individuals can decide to give each other certain rights. These rights may or may not include, for example, the right to publish something. In that situation, the individual ethic would flow from the collective ethic, just as the State says it does.

(*Pause.*)

I only mean it is a question you would have to deal with.

HOLLAR: I mean, it is not safe for me.

ANDERSON: (*Still misunderstanding*) Well yes, but for example, you could say that such an arrangement between a man and the State is a sort of contract, and it is the essence of a contract that both parties enter into it freely. And you have not entered into it freely. I mean, that would be one line of attack.

HOLLAR: It is not the main line. You see, to me the idea of an inherent right is intelligible. I believe that we have such rights, and they are paramount.

ANDERSON: Yes, I see you do, but how do you justify the assertion?

HOLLAR: I observe. I observe my son for example.

ANDERSON: Your son?

HOLLAR: For example.

(*Pause.*)

ANDERSON: Look, there's no need to stand out here. There's . . . no point. I was going to have a bath and change . . . meeting some of my colleagues later. . . .

(ANDERSON *moves to go but* HOLLAR *stops him with a touch on the arm.*)

HOLLAR: I am not a famous dissident. A writer, a scientist. . . .

ANDERSON: No.

HOLLAR: If I am picked up—on the way home, let us say—there is no fuss. A cleaner. I will be one of hundreds. It's all right. In the end it must change. But I have something to say—that is all. If I leave my statement behind, then it's O.K. You understand?

ANDERSON: Perhaps the correct thing for me to have done is not to have accepted their invitation to speak here. But I did accept it. It is a contract, as it were, freely entered into. And having accepted their hospitality I cannot in all conscience start smuggling. . . . It's just not ethical.

HOLLAR: But if you didn't know you were smuggling it—

ANDERSON: Smuggling entails knowledge.

HOLLAR: If I hid my thesis in your luggage, for instance.

ANDERSON: That's childish. Also, you could be getting me into trouble, and your quarrel is not with me. Your action would be unethical on your own terms—one man's dealings with another man. I am sorry.

(ANDERSON *goes back towards his door, which* HOLLAR *had left ajar.* HOLLAR *follows him.*)

HOLLAR: No, it is I who must apologize.

The man next door, is he one of your group?

ANDERSON: No. I don't know him.

(ANDERSON *opens his bedroom door. He turns as if to say good-bye.*)

HOLLAR: My bag.

ANDERSON: Oh yes.

(HOLLAR *follows* ANDERSON *into the room.*)

HOLLAR: You will have a bath . . . ?

ANDERSON: I thought I would.

(HOLLAR *turns into the bathroom.* ANDERSON *stays in the bedroom, surprised.*

*He hears the bath water being turned on. The bath water makes a rush of sound.* ANDERSON *enters the bathroom and sees* HOLLAR *sitting on the edge of the bath.*

*Interior bathroom.*)

HOLLAR: (*Quietly*) I have not yet made a copy.

ANDERSON: (*Loudly*) What?

142

(HOLLAR *goes up to* ANDERSON *and speaks close to* ANDERSON'*s ear. The bath taps make a loud background noise.*)

HOLLAR: I have not yet made a copy. I have a bad feeling about carrying this home. (*He indicates his envelope.*) I did not expect to take it away. I ask a favour. (*Smiles.*) Ethical.

ANDERSON: (*Quietly now*) What is it?

HOLLAR: Let me leave this here and you can bring it to my apartment tomorrow—I have a safe place for it there.

(HOLLAR *takes a piece of paper and a pencil from his pocket and starts writing his address in capital letters.*)

ANDERSON: But you know my time here is very crowded— (*Then he gives in.*) Do you live nearby?

HOLLAR: It is not far. I have written my address.

(HOLLAR *gives* ANDERSON *the paper.*)

ANDERSON: (*Forgetting to be quiet*) Do you seriously—

(HOLLAR *quietens* ANDERSON.)

Do you seriously expect to be searched on the way home?

HOLLAR: I don't know, but it is better to be careful. I wrote a letter to Mr Husak. Also some other things. So sometimes they follow me.

ANDERSON: But you weren't worried about bringing the thesis with you.

HOLLAR: No. If anybody watches me they want to know what books *you* give *me*.

ANDERSON: I see. Yes, all right, Hollar. I'll bring it tomorrow.

HOLLAR: Please don't leave it in your room when you go to eat. Take your briefcase.

(*They go back into the bedroom.* ANDERSON *puts* HOLLAR'*s envelope into his briefcase.*)

(*Normal voice*) So perhaps you will come and meet my wife.

ANDERSON: Yes. Should I telephone?

HOLLAR: Unfortunately my telephone is removed. I am home all day. Saturday.

ANDERSON: Oh yes.

HOLLAR: Good-bye.

ANDERSON: Good-bye.

(HOLLAR *goes to the door carrying his bag.*)

HOLLAR: I forgot—welcome to Prague.

(HOLLAR *leaves closing the door.*

143

ANDERSON *stands still for a few moments. Then he hears
footsteps approaching down the corridor. The footsteps appear
to stop outside his room. But then the door to the next room is
opened and the unseen man enters the room next door and
loudly closes the door behind him.*)


4. INT. ANDERSON'S ROOM. MORNING.

*Close-up of the colloquium brochure. It is lying on* ANDERSON's *table.
Then* ANDERSON *picks it up. His dress and appearance, and the light
outside the window, tell us that it is morning. Dressed to go out,*
ANDERSON *picks up his briefcase and leaves the room.
In the corridor he walks towards the lifts.
At the lifts he finds* CRISP *waiting.* ANDERSON *stands next to* CRISP
*silently for a few moments.*

ANDERSON: Good morning. (*Pause.*) Mr Crisp . . . my name is
Anderson. I'm a very great admirer of yours.

CRISP: (*Chewing gum*) Oh . . . ta.

ANDERSON: Good luck this afternoon.

CRISP: Thanks. Bloody useless, the lifts in this place.

ANDERSON: Are you all staying in this hotel?

(CRISP *doesn't seem to hear this.* CRISP *sees* BROADBENT
*emerging from a room.* BROADBENT *carries a zipped bag,* CRISP
*has a similar bag.*)

CRISP: (*Shouts*) Here you are, Roy—it's waiting for you.

(BROADBENT *arrives.*)

ANDERSON: Good morning. Good luck this afternoon.

BROADBENT: Right. Thanks. Are you over for the match?

ANDERSON: Yes. Well, partly. I've got my ticket.

(ANDERSON *takes out of his pocket the envelope he received
from the hotel* CLERK *and shows it.*)

CRISP: (*Quietly*) You didn't pull her, then?

BROADBENT: No chance.

CRISP: They don't trust you, do they?

BROADBENT: Well, they're right, aren't they? Remember Milan.

CRISP: (*Laughing*) Yeah—

(*The bell sounds to indicate that the lift is arriving.*)

About bloody time.

ANDERSON: I see from yesterday's paper that they've brought in
Jirasek for Vladislav.

BROADBENT: Yes, that's right. Six foot eight, they say.

ANDERSON: He's not very good in the air unless he's got lots of space.

(BROADBENT *looks at him curiously. The lift doors open and the three of them get in. There is no one else in the lift except the female* OPERATOR.

*Interior lift.*)

BROADBENT: You've seen him, have you?

ANDERSON: I've seen him twice. In the UFA Cup a few seasons ago. . . . I happened to be in Berlin for the Hegel Colloquium, er, bunfight. And then last season I was in Bratislava to receive an honorary degree.

CRISP: Tap his ankles for him. Teach him to be six foot eight.

BROADBENT: Leave off— (*He nods at the lift* OPERATOR.) You never know, do you?

CRISP: Yeah, maybe the lift's bugged.

ANDERSON: He scored both times from the same move, and came close twice more—

BROADBENT: Oh yes?

(*Pause.*)

ANDERSON: (*In a rush*) I realize it's none of my business—I mean you may think I'm an absolute ass, but—

(*Pause.*)

Look, if Halas takes a corner he's going to make it short— almost certainly—push it back to Deml or Kautsky, who pulls the defence out. Jirasek hangs about for the chip to the far post. They'll do the same thing from a set piece. Three or four times in the same match. *Really.* Short corners and free kicks.

(*The lift stops at the third floor.* BROADBENT *and* CRISP *are staring at* ANDERSON.)

(*Lamely.*) Anyway, that's why they've brought Jirasek back, in my opinion.

(*The lift doors open and* MCKENDRICK *gets in.* MCKENDRICK'S *manner is breezy and bright.*)

MCKENDRICK: Good morning! You've got together then?

ANDERSON: A colleague. Mr McKendrick . . .

MCKENDRICK: You're Crisp. (*He takes* CRISP'S *hand and shakes it.*) Bill McKendrick. I hear you're doing some very interesting work in Newcastle. Great stuff. I still like to think of myself as a bit of a left-winger at Stoke. Of course, my stuff is largely empirical—I leave epistemologial questions to the scholastics—eh, Anderson? (*He pokes* ANDERSON *in the ribs.*)

ANDERSON: McKendrick . . .

BROADBENT: Did you say *Stoke*?

(*The lift arives at the ground floor.*)

MCKENDRICK: (*To* BROADBENT) We've met, haven't we? Your face is familiar . . .

(BROADBENT, CRISP *and* MCKENDRICK *in close attendance leave the lift.* ANDERSON *is slow on the uptake but follows.*)

ANDERSON: McKendrick—?

MCKENDRICK: (*Prattling*) There's a choice of open forums tonight —neo-Hegelians or Quinian neo-Positivists. Which do you fancy? Pity Quine couldn't be here. And Hegel for that matter.

(MCKENDRICK *laughs brazenly in the lobby.* BROADBENT *and* CRISP *eye him warily.* ANDERSON *winces.*)


### 5. INT. THE COLLOQUIUM

*The general idea is that a lot of philosophers sit in a sort of theatre while on stage one of their number reads a paper from behind a lectern, with a* CHAIRMAN *in attendance behind him. The set up however is quite complicated. To one side are three glassed-in booths, each one containing 'simultaneous interpreters'. These interpreters have earphones and microphones. They also have a copy of the lecture being given. One of these interpreters is translating into Czech, another into French, another into German. The audience is furnished either with earphones or with those hand-held phones which are issued in theatres sometimes. Each of these phones can tune into any of the three interpreters depending upon the language of the listener. For our purposes it is better to have the hand-held phones.*

*It is important to the play, specifically to a later scene when* ANDERSON *is talking, that the hall and the audience should be substantial.*

*At the moment* ANDERSON *is in the audience, sitting next to* MCKENDRICK. MCKENDRICK *is still discomforted.* CHETWYN *is elsewhere in the audience.*

*We begin however with a large close-up of the speaker who is an American called* STONE. *After the first sentence or two of* STONE'*s speech, the camera will acquaint us with the situation. At different points during* STONE's *speech, there is conversation between* ANDERSON *and* MCKENDRICK. *In this script, these conversations are placed immediately after that part of* STONE's *speech which they will cover. This applies also to any other interpolations. Obviously,* STONE *does not pause to let these other things in.*

STONE: The confusion which often arises from the ambiguity of ordinary language raises special problems for a logical language. This is especially so when the ambiguity is not casual and inadvertent—but when it's contrived. In fact, the limitations of a logical language are likely to appear when we ask ourselves whether it can accommodate a literature, or whether poetry can be reduced to a logical language. It is here that deliberate ambiguity for effect makes problems.

ANDERSON: Perfectly understandable mistake.

STONE: Nor must we confuse ambiguity, furthermore, with mere synonymity. When we say that a politician ran for office, that is not an ambiguous statement, it is merely an instance of a word having different applications, literal, idiomatic and so on.

MCKENDRICK: I said I knew his face.

ANDERSON: Match of the Day.

STONE: The intent is clear in each application. The show ran well on Broadway. Native Dancer ran well at Kentucky, and so on. (*In the audience a Frenchman expresses dismay and bewilderment as his earphones give out a literal translation of 'a native dancer' running well at Kentucky. Likewise a German listener has the same problem.*)
And what about this word 'Well'? Again, it is applied as a qualifier with various intent—the show ran for a long time, the horse ran fast, and so on.

MCKENDRICK: So this pressing engagement of yours is a football match.

ANDERSON: A World Cup qualifier is not just a football match.

STONE: Again, there is no problem here so long as these variations are what I propose to call reliable. 'You eat well' says Mary to John, 'You cook well' says John to Mary. We know that when Mary says 'You *eat* well' she does not mean that John eats *skilfully.* Just as we know that when John says 'You cook

147

well' he does not mean that Mary cooks *abundantly*.

ANDERSON: But I'm sorry about missing your paper, I really am.

STONE: I say that we know this, but I mean only that our general experience indicates it. The qualifier takes its meaning from the contexual force of the verb it qualifies. But it is the mark of a sound theory that it should take account not merely of our general experience, but also of the particular experience, and not merely of the particular experience but also of the unique experience, and not merely of the unique experience but also of the hypothetical experience. It is when we consider the world of *possibilities*, hypothetical experience, that we get closer to ambiguity. 'You cook well' says John to Mary. 'You eat well' says Mary to John.

MCKENDRICK: Do you ever wonder whether all this is worthwhile?

ANDERSON: No.

MCKENDRICK: I know what you mean.

(CHETWYN *is twisting the knob on his translation phone, to try all this out in different languages. He is clearly bored. He looks at his watch.*)

STONE: No problems there. But I ask you to imagine a competition when what is being judged is table manners.

(*Insert* FRENCH INTERPRETER's *box—interior.*)

INTERPRETER: . . . bonne tenue à table . . .

STONE: John enters this competition and afterwards Mary says, 'Well, you certainly ate well!' Now Mary seems to be saying that John ate *skilfully—with refinement*. And again, I ask you to imagine a competition where the amount of food eaten is taken into account along with refinement of table manners. *Now* Mary says to John, 'Well, you didn't eat very well, but at least you ate well.'

INTERPRETER: Alors, vous n'avez pas bien mangé . . . mais . . .

(*All* INTERPRETERS *baffled by this.*)

STONE: Now clearly there is no way to tell whether Mary means that John ate abundantly but clumsily, or that John ate frugally but elegantly. Here we have a genuine ambiguity. To restate Mary's sentence in a logical language we would have to ask her what she meant.

MCKENDRICK: By the way, I've got you a copy of my paper.

ANDERSON: Oh, many thanks.

MCKENDRICK: It's not a long paper. You could read it comfortably during half-time.

(MCKENDRICK *gives* ANDERSON *his paper*.)

STONE: But this is to assume that Mary exists. Let us say she is a fictitious character in a story I have written. Very well, you say to me, the author, 'What did Mary mean?' Well I might reply—'I don't know what she meant. Her ambiguity makes the necessary point of my story.' And here I think the idea of a logical language which can *only* be unambiguous, breaks down.

(ANDERSON *opens his briefcase and puts* MCKENDRICK'S *paper into it. He fingers* HOLLAR'S *envelope and broods over it.* STONE *has concluded. He sits down to applause. The* CHAIRMAN, *who has been sitting behind him has stood up*.)

ANDERSON: I'm going to make a discreet exit—I've got a call to make before the match.

(ANDERSON *stands up*.)

CHAIRMAN: Yes—Professor Anderson I think . . . ?

(ANDERSON *is caught like a rabbit in the headlights.* MCKENDRICK *enjoys his predicament and becomes interested in how* ANDERSON *will deal with it*.)

ANDERSON: Ah . . . I would only like to offer Professor Stone the observation that language is not the only level of human communication, and perhaps not the most important level. Whereof we cannot speak, thereof we are by no means silent.

(MCKENDRICK *smiles* 'Bravo'.)

Verbal language is a technical refinement of our capacity for communication, rather than the *fons et origo* of that capacity. The likelihood is that language develops in an *ad hoc* way, so there is no reason to expect its development to be logical. (*A thought strikes him*.) The importance of language is overrated. It allows me and Professor Stone to show off a bit, and it is very useful for communicating detail—but the important truths are simple and monolithic. The essentials of a given situation speak for themselves, and language is as capable of obscuring the truth as of revealing it. Thank you.

(ANDERSON *edges his way out towards the door*.)

CHAIRMAN: (*Uncertainly*) Professor Stone . . .

STONE: Well, what was the question?

### 6. EXT. FRONT DOOR OF THE HOLLAR APARTMENT

*The apartment is one of two half-way up a large old building. The stairwell is dirty and uncared for. The* HOLLAR *front door is on a landing, and the front door of another flat is across the landing. Stairs go up and down.* ANDERSON *comes up the stairs and finds the right number on the door and rings the bell. He is carrying his briefcase.*

*All the men in this scene are Czech plainclothes* POLICEMEN. *They will be identified in this text merely by number.* MAN 3 *is the one in charge.* Man 1 comes to the door.

ANDERSON: I'm looking for Mr Hollar.

 (MAN 1 *shakes his head. He looks behind him.* MAN 2 *comes to the door.*)

MAN 2: (*In Czech*) Yes? Who are you?

ANDERSON: English? Um. Parlez-vous francais? Er. Spreckanzydoitch?

MAN 2: (*In German*) Deutch? Ein Bischen.

ANDERSON: Actually I don't. Does Mr Hollar live here? Apartment Hollar?

 (MAN 2 *speaks to somebody behind him.*)

MAN 2: (*In Czech*) An Englishman. Do you know him?

 (MRS HOLLAR *comes to the door. She is about the same age as* HOLLAR.)

ANDERSON: Mrs Hollar?

 (MRS HOLLAR *nods.*)

 Is your husband here? Pavel . . .

MRS HOLLAR: (*In Czech*) Pavel is arrested.

 (*Inside, behind the door,* MAN 3 *is heard shouting, in Czech.*)

MAN 3: (*Not seen*) What's going on there?

 (MAN 3 *comes to the door.*)

ANDERSON: I am looking for Mr Hollar. I am a friend from England. His Professor. My name is Anderson.

MAN 3. (*In English*) Not here. (*In Czech to* MRS HOLLAR.) He says he is a friend of your husband. Anderson.

ANDERSON: He was my student.

 (MRS HOLLAR *calls out.*)

MAN 3: (*In Czech*) Shut up.

ANDERSON: Student. Philosophy.

 (MRS HOLLAR *calls out.*)

MAN 3: Shut up.

(MAN 3 *and* MAN 2 *come out of the flat on to the landing,*
*closing the door behind them.*)

ANDERSON: I just came to see him. Just to say hello. For a
minute. I have a taxi waiting. Taxi.

MAN 3: Taxi.

ANDERSON: Yes. I can't stay.

MAN 3: (*In English*) Moment. O.K.

ANDERSON: I can't stay.

(MAN 3 *rings the bell of the adjacent flat. A rather scared*
*woman opens the door.* MAN 3 *asks, in Czech, to use the phone.*
MAN 3 *goes inside the other flat.* ANDERSON *begins to realize*
*the situation.*)

Well, look, if you don't mind—I'm on my way to—an
engagement. . . .

MAN 2: (*In Czech*) Stay here.

(*Pause.* ANDERSON *looks at his watch. Then from inside the flat*
MRS HOLLAR *is shouting in Czech.*)

MRS HOLLAR: (*Unseen*) I'm entitled to a witness of my choice.

(*The door is opened violently and immediately slammed.*
ANDERSON *becomes agitated.*)

ANDERSON: What's going on in there?

MAN 2: (*In Czech*) Stay here, he won't be a minute.

(ANDERSON *can hear* MRS HOLLAR *shouting.*)

ANDERSON: Now look here—

(ANDERSON *rings the doorbell.*
*The door is opened by* MAN 4.)

I demand to speak to Mrs Hollar.

(*Upstairs and downstairs doors are opening and people are*
*shouting, in Czech 'What's going on?' And so on. There is also*
*shouting from inside the flat.* MAN 2 *shouts up and down the*
*staircase, in Czech.*)

MAN 2: (*In Czech*) Go inside!

ANDERSON: Now look here, I am the J. S. Mill Professor of
Ethics at the University of Cambridge and I demand that I
am allowed to leave or to telephone the British Ambassador!

MAN 4: (*In Czech*) Bring him inside.

MAN 2: (*In Czech*) In.

(*He pushes* ANDERSON *into the flat. Interior flat. The hallway.*
*Inside it is apparent that the front door leads to more than one*

*flat. Off the very small dirty hall there is a kitchen, a lavatory and two other doors, not counting the door to the* HOLLAR *rooms.*)

MAN 4: (*In Czech*) Stay with him.

(*The* HOLLAR *interior door is opened from inside by* MRS HOLLAR.)

MRS HOLLAR: (*In Czech*) If he's my witness he's allowed in here.

MAN 4: (*In Czech*) Go inside—he's not your witness.

(MAN 4 *pushes* MRS HOLLAR *inside and closes the door from within. This leaves* ANDERSON *and* MAN 2 *in the little hall. Another door now opens, and a small girl, poorly dressed, looks round it. She is jerked back out of sight by someone and the door is pulled closed. The* HOLLAR *door is flung open again, by* MRS HOLLAR.)

MRS HOLLAR: (*In Czech*) I want this door open.

MAN 2: (*In Czech*) Leave it open then. He'll be back in a minute.

(MAN 4 *disappears back inside the flat.* MRS HOLLAR *is heard.*)

MRS HOLLAR: (*Unseen. In Czech*) Bastards.

(ANDERSON *stands in the hallway. He can hear* MRS HOLLAR *starting to cry.* ANDERSON *looks completely out of his depth.*)

ANDERSON: My God. . . .

(*Then the doorbell rings.* MAN 2 *opens it to let in* MAN 3.)

MAN 2: (*In Czech*) We had to come in to shut her up.

MAN 3: (*In Czech*) Well, he's coming over. (*In English to* ANDERSON.) Captain coming. Speak English.

ANDERSON: I would like to telephone the British Ambassador.

MAN 3: (*In English*) O.K. Captain coming.

ANDERSON: How long will he be? I have an appointment. (*He looks at his watch.*) Yes, by God! I do have an engagement and it starts in half an hour—

MAN 3: (*In English*) Please.

(*A lavatory flushes. From the other interior door an* OLD MAN *comes out.* MAN 3 *nods curtly at the* OLD MAN. *The* OLD MAN *shuffles by looking at* ANDERSON. MAN 3 *becomes uneasy at being in the traffic. He decides to bring* ANDERSON *inside the flat. He does so.*

*Interior* HOLLAR'*s room. There are two connecting rooms. Beyond this room is a door leading to a bedroom. This door is open. The rooms seem full of people. The rooms are small and shabby. They are being thoroughly searched, and obviously have been in this process for hours. The searchers do not spoil or destroy anything. There are no torn cushions or anything like that. However, the floor of the first room is almost covered in books. The bookcases which line perhaps two of the walls are empty. The rug could be rolled up, and there could be one or two floorboards up.*

*MAN 1 is going through the books, leafing through each one and looking along the spine. He is starting to put books back on the shelves one by one. MAN 5 has emptied drawers of their contents and is going through a pile of papers. MRS HOLLAR stands in the doorway between the two rooms. Beyond her MAN 2 can be seen searching. [MAN 4 is out of sight in the bedroom.] MAN 3 indicates a chair on which ANDERSON should sit. ANDERSON sits putting his briefcase on the floor by his feet. He looks around. He sees a clock showing 2.35.*

*Mix to clock showing 2.55.*

*ANDERSON is where he was. MAN 1 is still on the books. MAN 5 is still looking through papers. MAN 3 is examining the inside of a radio set.*

*Voices are heard faintly on the stairs. There is a man remonstrating. A woman's voice too.*

*The doorbell rings.*

*MAN 3 leaves the room, closing the door. ANDERSON hears him go to the front door. There is some conversation. The front door closes again and MAN 3 re-enters the room.*)

MAN 3: (*In English to ANDERSON*) Taxi.

ANDERSON: Oh—I forgot him. Dear me.

MAN 3: O.K.

ANDERSON: I must pay him.

(ANDERSON *takes out his wallet.* MAN 3 *takes it from him without snatching.*)

MAN 3: O.K.

(MAN 3 *looks through the wallet.*)

ANDERSON: Give that back— (*Furious*) Now, you listen to me— this has gone on quite long enough—I demand—to be allowed to leave. . . .

(ANDERSON *has stood up.* MAN 3 *gently pushes him back into the chair. In* ANDERSON'S *wallet* MAN 3 *finds his envelope and*

*discovers the football ticket. He puts it back. He looks*
*sympathetically at* ANDERSON.)

MAN 3: (*In Czech*) The old boy's got a ticket for the England
match. No wonder he's furious. (*He gives the wallet back to*
ANDERSON. *In English*.) Taxi O.K. No money. He go.
Football no good.

ANDERSON: Serve me right.

MAN 5: (*In Czech*) It's on the radio. Let him have it on.
(MAN 3 *returns to the radio and turns it on.*
MRS HOLLAR *enters quickly from the bedroom and turns it off.*)

MRS HOLLAR: (*In Czech*) That's my radio.

MAN 3: (*In Czech*) Your friend wants to listen to the match.
(MRS HOLLAR *looks at* ANDERSON. *She turns the radio on.*
*The radio is talking about the match which is just about to*
*begin*.)

MAN 3: (*In English*) Is good. O.K.?
(ANDERSON, *listening, realizes that the radio is listing the names*
*of the English team.*
*Then the match begins.*
*Mix to:*
*The same situation about half an hour later. The radio is still*
*on.* MAN I *is still on the books. He has put aside three or four*
*English books.* MAN 5 *has disappeared.* MAN 2 *is sorting out the*
*fluff from a carpet sweeper.* MAN 4 *is standing on a chair*
*examining the inside of a ventilation grating.*
ANDERSON *gets up off his chair and starts to walk towards the*
*bedroom. The three* MEN *in the room look up but don't stop him.*
ANDERSON *enters the bedroom.*
*Interior bedroom.*
MAN 3 *is going through pockets in a wardrobe.* MAN 5 *is*
*looking under floorboards.* MRS HOLLAR *is sitting on the bed*
*watching them.*)

ANDERSON: It's half-past three. I demand to be allowed to leave
or to telephone the British—

MAN 3: Please—too slow.

ANDERSON: I demand to leave—

MAN 3: O.K. Who wins football?

ANDERSON: (*Pause*) No score.
(*The doorbell goes.*

MAN 3 *goes into the other room and to the door.* ANDERSON
*follows him as far as the other room. On the way through*
MAN 3 *signals to turn off the radio.* MAN 2 *turns off the radio.*
MRS HOLLAR *comes in and turns the radio on.*)

MRS HOLLAR: (*In Czech*) Show me where it says I can't listen to
my own radio.

(MAN 3 *returns from the front door with* MAN 6. MAN 6 *enters
the room saying:*)

MAN 6: (*In Czech*) I said don't let him leave—I didn't say bring
him inside. (*To* ANDERSON *in English.*) Professor Anderson?
I'm sorry your friend Mr Hollar has got himself into
trouble.

ANDERSON: Thank Christ—now listen to me—I am a professor of
philosophy. I am a guest of the Czechoslovakian government.
I might almost say an honoured guest. I have been invited
to speak at the Colloquium in Prague. My connections in
England reach up to the highest in the land—

MAN 6: Do you know the Queen?

ANDERSON: Certainly. (*But he has rushed into that.*) No, I do not
know the Queen—but I speak the truth when I say that I
am personally acquainted with two members of the
government, one of whom has been to my house, and I
assure you that unless I am allowed to leave this building
immediately there is going to be a major incident about the
way my liberty has been impeded by your men. I do not
know what they are doing here, I do not care what they are
doing here—

MAN 6: Excuse me. Professor. There is some mistake. I thought
you were here as a friend of the Hollar family.

ANDERSON: I know Pavel Hollar, certainly.

MAN 6: Absolutely. You are here as a friend, at Mrs Hollar's
request.

ANDERSON: I just dropped in to—what do you mean?

MAN 6: Mr Hollar unfortunately has been arrested for a serious
crime against the State. It is usual for the home of an
accused person to be searched for evidence, and so on. I am
sure the same thing happens in your country. Well, under
our law Mrs Hollar is entitled to have a friendly witness
present during the search. To be frank she is entitled to two

witnesses. So if, for example, an expensive vase is broken by mistake, and the police claim it was broken before, it will not just be her word against theirs. And so on. I think you will agree that's fair.

ANDERSON: Well?

MAN 6: Well, my understanding is that she asked you to be her witness. (*In Czech to* MRS HOLLAR.) Did you ask him to be your witness?

MRS HOLLAR: (*In Czech*) Yes, I did.

MAN 6: (*In English to* ANDERSON) Yes. Exactly so. (*Pause.*) You are Mr Hollar's friend, aren't you?

ANDERSON: I taught him in Cambridge after he left Czechoslovakia.

MAN 6: A brave man.

ANDERSON: Yes . . . a change of language . . . and culture . . .

MAN 6: He walked across a minefield. In 1962. Brave.

ANDERSON: Perhaps he was simply desperate.

MAN 6: Perhaps a little ungrateful. The State, you know, educated him, fed him, for eighteen years. 'Thank you very much—good-bye.'

ANDERSON: Well he came back, in the Spring of sixty-eight.

MAN 6: Oh yes.

ANDERSON: A miscalculation.

MAN 6: How do you mean?

ANDERSON: Well, really . . . there are a lot of things wrong in England but it is still not 'a serious crime against the State' to put forward a philosophical view which does not find favour with the Government.

MAN 6: Professor. . . . Hollar is charged with currency offences. There is a black market in hard currency. It is illegal. We do not have laws about philosophy. He is an ordinary criminal.

(*Pause.*

*The radio commentary has continued softly. But in this pause it changes pitch. It is clear to* ANDERSON, *and to us, that something particular has occurred in the match.* MAN 6 *is listening.*)

(*In English.*) Penalty. (*He listens for a moment.*) For us, I'm afraid.

ANDERSON: Yes, I can hear.

*(This is because it is clear from the crowd noise that it's a penalty for the home side.* MAN 6 *listens again.)*

MAN 6: *(In English)* Broadbent—a bad tackle when Deml had a certain goal . . . a what you call it?—a necessary foul.

ANDERSON: A professional foul.

MAN 6: Yes.

*(On the radio the goal is scored. This is perfectly clear from the the crowd reaction.)*

Not good for you.

*(*MAN 6 *turns off the radio. Pause.* MAN 6 *considers* ANDERSON.*)*

So you have had a philosophical discussion with Hollar.

ANDERSON: I believe you implied that I was free to go. *(He stands up.)* I am quite sure you know that Hollar visited me at my hotel last night. It was a social call, which I was returning when I walked into this. And furthermore, I understood nothing about being a witness—I was prevented from leaving. I only came to say hello, and meet Pavel's wife, on my way to the football—

MAN 6: *(With surprise)* So you came to Czechoslovakia to go to the football match, Professor?

*(This rattles* ANDERSON.*)*

ANDERSON: Certainly not. Well, the afternoon of the Colloquium was devoted to—well, it was not a condition of my invitation that I should attend all the sessions. *(Pause.)* I was invited to *speak*, not to listen. I am speaking tomorrow morning.

MAN 6: Why should I know Hollar visited you at the hotel?

ANDERSON: He told me he was often followed.

MAN 6: Well, when a man is known to be engaged in meeting foreigners to buy currency—

ANDERSON: I don't believe any of that—he was being harassed because of his letter to Husak—

MAN 6: A letter to President Husak? What sort of letter?

ANDERSON: *(Flustered)* Your people knew about it—

MAN 6: It is not a crime to write to the President—

ANDERSON: No doubt that depends on what is written.

MAN 6: You mean he wrote some kind of slander?

ANDERSON: *(Heatedly)* I insist on leaving now.

MAN 6: Of course. You know, your taxi driver has made a complaint against you.

157

ANDERSON: What are you talking about?

MAN 6: He never got paid.

ANDERSON: Yes, I'm sorry but—

MAN 6: You are not to blame. My officer told him to go.

ANDERSON: Yes, that's right.

MAN 6: Still, he is very unhappy. You told him you would be five minutes you were delivering something—

ANDERSON: How could I have told him that? I don't speak Czech.

MAN 6: You showed him five on your watch, and you did all the things people do when they talk to each other without a language. He was quite certain you were delivering something in your briefcase.

(*Pause.*)

ANDERSON: Yes. All right. But it was not money.

MAN 6: Of course not. You are not a criminal.

ANDERSON: Quite so. I promised to bring Pavel one or two of the Colloquium papers. He naturally has an interest in philosophy and I assume it is not illegal.

MAN 6: Naturally not. Then you won't mind showing me.

(ANDERSON *hesitates then opens the briefcase and takes out* MCKENDRICK's *paper and his own and passes them over.* MAN 6 *takes them and reads their English titles.*)

'Ethical Fictions as Ethical Foundations' . . . 'Philosophy and the Catastrophe Theory'.

(MAN 6 *gives the papers back to* ANDERSON.)

MAN 6: You wish to go to the football match? You will see twenty minutes, perhaps more.

ANDERSON: No. I'm going back to the university, to the Colloquium.

MRS HOLLAR: (*In Czech*) Is he leaving?

MAN 6: Mrs Hollar would like you to remain.

ANDERSON: (*To* MRS HOLLAR) No, I'm sorry. (*A thought strikes him.*) If you spoke to the taxi driver you would have known perfectly well I was going to the England match.

(MAN 6 *doesn't reply to this either in word or expression.* ANDERSON *closes his briefcase.*

*The doorbell rings and* MAN 3 *goes to open the door.*

*From the bedroom* MAN 5 *enters with a small parcel wrapped*

158

*in old newspaper.*)

MAN 5: (*In Czech*) I found this, Chief, under the floorboards.
(MAN 5 *gives the parcel to* MAN 6 *who unwraps it to reveal a bundle of American dollars.*

MRS HOLLAR *watches this with disbelief and there is an outburst.*)

MRS HOLLAR: (*In Czech*) He's lying! (*To* ANDERSON.) It's a lie—
*The door reopens for* MAN 3. SACHA HOLLAR, *aged ten, comes in with him. He is rather a tough little boy. He runs across to his mother, who is crying and shouting, and embraces her. It is rather as though he were a small adult comforting her.*)

ANDERSON: Oh my God . . . Mrs Hollar . . .
(ANDERSON, *out of his depth and afraid, decides abruptly to leave and does so.* MAN 3 *isn't sure whether to let him go but* MAN 6 *nods at him and* ANDERSON *leaves.*)

7. INT. HOTEL CORRIDOR. EVENING

ANDERSON *approaches his room. He is worn out. When he gets to his door and fumbles with his key he realizes that he can hear a voice in the room next door to his. He puts his ear to this other door.*

GRAYSON: (*Inside*) Yes, a new top for the running piece—O.K.—
Prague, Saturday.
(GRAYSON *speaks not particularly slowly but with great deliberation enunciating every consonant and splitting syllables up where necessary for clarity. He is, of course, dictating to a fast typist.*)
There'll be Czechs bouncing in the streets of Prague tonight as bankruptcy stares English football in the face, stop, new par.
(ANDERSON *knocks on the door.*)
(*Inside.*) It's open!
(ANDERSON *opens the door and looks into the room.*
*Interior room. It is of course a room very like* ANDERSON'S *own room, if not identical. Its occupant, the man we had seen leave the room earlier is* GRAYSON, *a sports reporter from England. He is on the telephone as* ANDERSON *cautiously enters the room.*)
Make no mistake, comma, the four-goal credit which these slick Slovaks netted here this afternoon will keep them in the black through the second leg of the World Cup Eliminator

at Wembley next month, stop. New par— (*To* ANDERSON.) Yes? (*Into phone.*) You can bank on it.

ANDERSON: I'm next door.

GRAYSON: (*Into phone*) —bank on it. New par— (*To* ANDERSON.) Look, can you come back? (*Into phone.*) But for some determined saving by third-choice Jim Bart in the injury hyphen jinxed England goal, we would have been overdrawn by four more when the books were closed, stop. Maybe Napoleon was wrong when he said we were a nation of shopkeepers, stop. Today England looked like a nation of goalkeepers, stop. Davey, Petherbridge and Shell all made saves on the line. New par.

ANDERSON: Do you mind if I listen—I missed the match.

(GRAYSON *waves him to a chair.* ANDERSON *sits on a chair next to a door which is in fact a connecting door into the next room. Not* ANDERSON's *own room but the room on the other side of* GRAYSON's *room.*)

GRAYSON: (*Into phone*) Dickenson and Pratt were mostly left standing by Wolker, with a W, and Deml, D dog, E Edward, M mother, L London—who could go round the halls as a telepathy act, stop. Only Crisp looked as if he had a future outside Madame Tussaud's—a.u.d.s.—stop. He laid on the two best chances, comma, both wasted by Pratt who skied one and stubbed his toe on the other, stop. Crisp's, apostrophe s. comment from where I was sitting looked salt and vinegar flavoured . . .

(ANDERSON *has become aware that another voice is cutting in from the next room. The door between the two rooms is not quite closed. During* GRAYSON's *last speech* ANDERSON *gently pushes open the door and looks behind him and realizes that a colleague of* GRAYSON's *is also dictating in the next room.*

ANDERSON *stands up and looks into the next room and is drawn into it by the rival report.*

*This room belongs to* CHAMBERLAIN.

*Interior* CHAMBERLAIN's *room.* CHAMBERLAIN *on phone.*)

CHAMBERLAIN: Wilson, who would like to be thought the big bad man of the English defence merely looked slow-footed and slow-witted stop. Deml—D.E.M. mother L.—Deml got round him five times on the trot, bracket, literally, close bracket, using the same swerve, comma, making Wilson look elephantine in everything but memory, stop. On the fifth occasion there was nothing to prevent Deml scoring except what Broadbent took it on himself to do, which was to scythe Deml down from behind, stop. Halas scored from the penalty, stop.

(ANDERSON *sighs and sits down on the equivalent chair in* CHAMBERLAIN's *room.* CHAMBERLAIN *sees him.*)

Can I help you—?

ANDERSON: Sorry—I'm from next door.

CHAMBERLAIN: (*Into phone*) New paragraph— (*To* ANDERSON.) I won't be long— (*Into phone.*) This goal emboldened the Czechs to move Bartok, like the composer, forward and risk the consequences, stop. Ten minutes later, just before half time, comma, he was the man left over to collect a short corner from Halas and it was his chip which Jirasek rose to meet for a simple goal at the far post—

ANDERSON: I knew it!

(CHAMBERLAIN *turns to look at him.*)

CHAMBERLAIN: (*Into phone*) New paragraph. As with tragic opera, things got worse after the interval . . .

(ANDERSON *has stood up to leave. He leaves through* GRAYSON's *room.* GRAYSON *is on the phone saying:*)

GRAYSON: (*Into the phone*) . . . Jirasek, unmarked at the far post, flapped into the air like a great stork, and rising a yard higher than Bart's outstretched hands, he put Czechoslovakia on the road to victory.

(ANDERSON *leaves the room without looking at* GRAYSON *or being noticed.*)


8. INT. HOTEL DINING ROOM

*The cut is to gay Czech music.*

*The dining room has a stage. A small group of Czech musicians and singers in the tourist version of peasant costume is performing.*

*It is evening. At one of the tables* STONE, *the American, and a* FRENCH-MAN *are sitting next to each other and sharing the table are* ANDERSON, MCKENDRICK *and* CHETWYN. *The three of them are, for different reasons, subdued.* STONE *is unsubdued. They are reaching the end of the meal.*

STONE: Hell's bells. Don't you understand English? When I say to you, 'Tell me what you mean,' you can only reply, 'I would wish to say so and so.' 'Never mind what you would wish to say,' I reply. 'Tell me what you *mean*.'

FRENCHMAN: Mais oui, but if you ask me in French, you must say, 'Qu'est-ce que vous voulez dire?'—'What is that which you wish to say?' Naturellement, it is in order for me to reply, 'Je veux dire etcetera.'

STONE: (*Excitedly*) But you are making *my* point—don't you see?

MCKENDRICK: What do you think the chances are of meeting a free and easy woman in a place like this?

STONE: I *can't* ask you in French.

MCKENDRICK: I don't mean free, necessarily.

FRENCHMAN: Pourquoi non? Qu'est-ce que vous voulez dire? Voila!—now I have asked you.

CHETWYN: You don't often see goose on an English menu. (CHETWYN *is the last to finish his main course. They have all eaten the main course. There are drinks and cups of coffee on the table.*)

STONE: The French have no verb meaning 'I mean'.

CHETWYN: Why's that I wonder.

STONE: They just don't.

CHETWYN: People are always eating goose in Dickens.

MCKENDRICK: Do you think it will be safe?

FRENCHMAN: Par exemple. Je vous dis, 'Qu'est-ce que vous voulez dire?'

MCKENDRICK: I mean one wouldn't want to be photographed through a two-way mirror.

STONE: I don't want to ask you what you would wish to say. I want to ask you what you *mean*. Let's assume there is a difference.

ANDERSON: We do have goose liver. What do they do with the rest of the goose?

STONE: Now assume that you say one but mean the other.

FRENCHMAN: Je dis quelque chose, mais je veux dire—

STONE: Right.

MCKENDRICK: (*To* STONE) Excuse me, Brad.

STONE: Yes?

MCKENDRICK: You eat well but you're a lousy eater.

(*This is a fair comment.* STONE *has spoken with his mouth full of bread, cake, coffee, etc., and he is generally messy about it.* STONE *smiles forgivingly but hardly pauses.*)

STONE: Excuse us.

FRENCHMAN: A bientôt.

(STONE *and the* FRENCHMAN *get up to leave.*)

STONE: (*Leaving*) You see, what you've got is an incorrect statement which when corrected looks like itself.

(*There is a pause.*)

MCKENDRICK: Did you have a chance to read my paper?

ANDERSON: I only had time to glance at it. I look forward to reading it carefully.

CHETWYN: I read it.

ANDERSON: Weren't you there for it?

MCKENDRICK: No, he sloped off for the afternoon.

ANDERSON: Well, you sly devil, Chetwyn. I bet you had a depressing afternoon. It makes the heart sick, doesn't it.

CHETWYN: Yes, it does rather. We don't know we've been born.

MCKENDRICK: He wasn't at the football match.

CHETWYN: Oh—is that where you were?

ANDERSON: No, I got distracted.

MCKENDRICK: He's being mysterious. I think it's a woman.

ANDERSON: (*To* CHETWYN) What were you doing?

CHETWYN: I was meeting some friends.

MCKENDRICK: He's being mysterious. I don't think it's a woman.

CHETWYN: I have friends here, that's all.

ANDERSON: (*To* MCKENDRICK) Was your paper well received?

MCKENDRICK: No. They didn't get it. I could tell from the questions that there'd been some kind of communications failure.

ANDERSON: The translation phones?

MCKENDRICK: No, no—they simply didn't understand the line of argument. Most of them had never heard of catastrophe theory, so they weren't ready for what is admittedly an audacious application of it.

ANDERSON: I must admit I'm not absolutely clear about it.

MCKENDRICK: It's like a reverse gear—no—it's like a breaking point. The mistake that people make is, they think a moral principle is indefinitely extendible, that it holds good for any

163

situation, a straight line cutting across the graph of our actual situation—here you are, you see— (*He uses a knife to score a line in front of him straight across the table cloth, left to right in front of him.*) 'Morality' down there; running parallel to 'Immorality' up here— (*He scores a parallel line.*) —and never the twain shall meet. They think that is what a principle means.

ANDERSON: And isn't it?

MCKENDRICK: No. The two lines are on the same plane. (*He holds out his flat hand, palm down, above the scored lines.*) They're the edges of the same plane—it's in three dimensions, you see—and if you twist the plane in a certain way, into what we call the catastrophe curve, you get a model of the sort of behaviour we find in the real world. There's a point—the catastrophe point—where your progress along one line of behaviour jumps you into the opposite line; the principle reverses itself at the point where a rational man would abandon it.

CHETWYN: Then it's not a principle.

MCKENDRICK: There aren't any principles in your sense. There are only a lot of principled people trying to behave as if there were.

ANDERSON: That's the same thing, surely.

MCKENDRICK: You're a worse case than Chetwyn and his primitive Greeks. At least he has the excuse of *believing* in goodness and beauty. You know they're fictions but you're so hung up on them you want to treat them as if they were God-given absolutes.

ANDERSON: I don't see how else they would have any practical value—

MCKENDRICK: So you end up using a moral principle as your excuse for acting against a moral interest. It's a sort of funk—

(ANDERSON, *under pressure, slams his cup back on to its saucer in a very uncharacteristic and surprising way. His anger is all the more alarming for that.*)

ANDERSON: You make your points altogether too easily, McKendrick. What need have you of moral courage when your principles reverse themselves so conveniently?

MCKENDRICK: All right! I've gone too far. As usual. Sorry. Let's talk about something else. There's quite an attractive woman hanging about outside, loitering in the vestibule.

(*The dining room door offers a view of the lobby.*)

Do you think it is a trap? My wife said to me—now, Bill, don't do anything daft, you know what you're like, if a blonde knocked on your door with the top three buttons of her police uniform undone and asked for a cup of sugar you'd convince yourself she was a bus conductress brewing up in the next room.

ANDERSON: (*Chastened*) I'm sorry . . . you're right up to a point. There would be no moral dilemmas if moral principles worked in straight lines and never crossed each other. One meets test situations which have troubled much cleverer men than us.

CHETWYN: A good rule, I find, is to try them out on men much *less* clever than us. I often ask my son what *he* thinks.

ANDERSON: Your son?

CHETWYN: Yes. He's eight.

MCKENDRICK: She's definitely glancing this way—seriously, do you think one could chat her up?

(ANDERSON *turns round to look through the door and we see now that the woman is* MRS HOLLAR.)

ANDERSON: Excuse me.

(*He gets up and starts to leave but then comes back immediately and takes his briefcase from under the table and then leaves. We stay with the table.* MCKENDRICK *watches* ANDERSON *meet* MRS HOLLAR *and shake her hand and they disappear.*)

MCKENDRICK: Bloody hell, it *was* a woman. Crafty old beggar.


9. EXT. STREET. NIGHT

ANDERSON *and* MRS HOLLAR *walking.*

*A park. A park bench.* SACHA HOLLAR *sitting on the bench.* ANDERSON *and* MRS HOLLAR *arrive.*

MRS HOLLAR: (*In Czech*) Here he is. (*To* ANDERSON.) Sacha. (*In Czech.*) Thank him for coming.

SACHA: She is saying thank you that you come.

MRS HOLLAR: (*In Czech*) We're sorry to bother him.

SACHA: She is saying sorry for the trouble.

ANDERSON: No, no I am sorry about . . . everything. Do you learn English at school?

SACHA: Yes. I am learning English two years. With my father also.

ANDERSON: You are very good.

SACHA: Not good. You are a friend of my father. Thank you.

ANDERSON: I'm afraid I've done nothing.

SACHA: You have his writing?

ANDERSON: His thesis? Yes. It's in here. (*He indicates his briefcase.*)

SACHA: (*In Czech*) It's all right, he's still got it.

(MRS HOLLAR *nods.*)

MRS HOLLAR: (*In Czech*) Tell him I didn't know who he was today.

SACHA: My mother is not knowing who you are, tomorrow at the apartment.

ANDERSON: Today.

SACHA: Today. Pardon. So she is saying, 'Come here! Come here! Come inside the apartment!' Because she is not knowing. My father is not telling her. He is telling me only.

ANDERSON: I see. What did he tell you?

SACHA: He will go see his friend the English professor. He is taking the writing.

ANDERSON: I see. Did he return home last night?

SACHA: No. He is arrested outside hotel. Then in the night they come to make search.

ANDERSON: Had they been there all night?

SACHA: At eleven o'clock they are coming. They search twenty hours.

ANDERSON: My God.

SACHA: In morning I go to Bartolomesskaya to be seeing him.

MRS HOLLAR: (*Explains*) Police.

SACHA: But I am not seeing him. They say go home. I am waiting. Then I am going home. Then I am seeing you.

ANDERSON: What were they looking for?

SACHA: (*Shrugs*) Western books. Also my father is writing things. Letters, politics, philosophy. They find nothing. Some English books they don't like but really nothing. But the dollars, of course, they pretend to find.

(MRS HOLLAR *hears the word dollars.*)

MRS HOLLAR: (*In Czech*) Tell him the dollars were put there by the police.

SACHA: Not my father's dollars. He is having no monies.

ANDERSON: Yes. I know.

SACHA: They must arrest him for dollars because he does nothing. No bad things. He is signing something. So they are making trouble.

ANDERSON: Yes.

MRS HOLLAR: (*In Czech*) Tell him about Jan.

SACHA: You must give back my father's thesis. Not now. The next days. My mother cannot take it.

ANDERSON: He asked me to take it to England.

SACHA: Not possible now. But thank you.

ANDERSON: He asked me to take it.

SACHA: Not possible. Now they search you, I think. At the aeroport. Because they are seeing you coming to the apartment and you have too much contact. Maybe they are seeing us now.

(ANDERSON *looks around him.*)

Is possible.

ANDERSON: (*Uncomfortably*) I ought to tell you . . . (*Quickly.*) I came to the apartment to give the thesis back. I refused him. But he was afraid he might be stopped—I thought he just meant searched, not arrested—

SACHA: Too quick—too quick—

(*Pause.*)

ANDERSON: What do you want me to do?

SACHA: My father's friend—he is coming to Philosophy Congress today.

ANDERSON: Tomorrow.

SACHA: Yes tomorrow. You give him the writing. Is called Jan. Is O.K. Good friend.

(ANDERSON *nods.*)

ANDERSON: Jan.

SACHA: (*In Czech*) He'll bring it to the university hall for Jan tomorrow. (SACHA *stands up.*) We go home now.

(MRS HOLLAR *gets up and shakes hands with* ANDERSON.)

ANDERSON: I'm sorry . . . What will happen to him?

MRS HOLLAR: (*In Czech*) What was that?

SACHA: (*In Czech*) He wants to know what will happen to Daddy.

MRS HOLLAR: Ruzyne.

SACHA: That is the prison. Ruzyne.

(*Pause.*)

ANDERSON: I will, of course, try to help in England. I'll write letters. The Czech Ambassador . . . I have friends, too, in our government—

(ANDERSON *realizes that the boy has started to cry. He is specially taken aback because he has been talking to him like an adult.*)

Now listen—I am personally friendly with important people —the Minister of Education—people like that.

MRS HOLLAR: (*In Czech but to* ANDERSON) Please help Pavel—

ANDERSON: Mrs Hollar—I will do everything I can for him.

(*He watches* MRS HOLLAR *and* SACHA *walk away into the dark.*)

10. INT. ANDERSON'S ROOM. NIGHT

ANDERSON *is lying fully dressed on the bed. His eyes open. Only light from the window. There are faint voices from* GRAYSON's *room. After a while* ANDERSON *gets up and leaves his room and knocks on* GRAYSON's *door.*

*Exterior* GRAYSON's *room.*

GRAYSON *opens his door.*

GRAYSON: Oh hello. Sorry, are we making too much noise?

ANDERSON: No, it's all right, but I heard you were still up and I wondered if I could ask a favour of you. I wonder if I could borrow your typewriter.

GRAYSON: My typewriter?

ANDERSON: Yes.

GRAYSON: Well, I'm leaving in the morning.

ANDERSON: I'll let you have it back first thing. I'm leaving on the afternoon plane myself.

GRAYSON: Oh—all right then.

ANDERSON: That's most kind.

(*During the above the voices from the room have been semi-audible.*

MCKENDRICK's *voice, rather drunk, but articulate, is heard.*)

MCKENDRICK: (*His voice only, heard underneath the above dialogue*) Now, listen to me, I'm a professional philosopher. You'll do well to listen to what I have to say.

ANDERSON: That sounds as if you've got McKendrick in there.

GRAYSON: Oh—is he one of yours?

ANDERSON: I wouldn't put it like that.

GRAYSON: He's getting as tight as a tick.

ANDERSON: Yes.

GRAYSON: You couldn't collect him, could you? He's going to get clouted in a minute.

ANDERSON: Go ahead and clout him, if you like.

GRAYSON: It's not me. It's Broadbent and a couple of the lads. Your pal sort of latched on to us in the bar. He really ought to be getting home.

ANDERSON: I'll see what I can do.

(ANDERSON *follows* GRAYSON *into the room.*)

MCKENDRICK: How can you expect the kids to be little gentlemen when their heroes behave like yobs—answer me that—no— you haven't answered my question—if you've got yobs on the fields you're going to have yobs on the terraces.

(*Interior* GRAYSON'*s room.*

MCKENDRICK *is the only person standing up. He is holding court, with a bottle of whisky in one hand and his glass in the other. Around this small room are* BROADBENT, CRISP, CHAMBERLAIN, *and perhaps one or two members of the England squad. Signs of a bottle party.*)

GRAYSON: (*Closing his door*) I thought philosophers were quiet, studious sort of people.

ANDERSON: Well, some of us are.

MCKENDRICK: (*Shouts*) Anderson! You're the very man I want to see! We're having a philosophical discussion about the yob ethics of professional footballers—

BROADBENT: You want to watch it, mate.

MCKENDRICK: Roy here is sensitive because he gave away a penalty today, by a deliberate foul. To stop a certain goal he hacked a chap down. After all, a penalty might be saved and broken legs are quite rare—

(BROADBENT *stands up but* MCKENDRICK *pacifies him with a gesture.*)

it's perfectly all right—you were adopting the utilitarian values of the game, for the good of the team, for England! But I'm not talking about particular acts of expediency. No, I'm talking about the whole *ethos*.

ANDERSON: McKendrick, don't you think, it's about time we retired?

MCKENDRICK: (*Ignoring him*) Now, I've played soccer for years. Years and *years*. I played soccer from the age of *eight* until I was *thirteen*. At which point I went to a rugger school. Even so, Tommy here will tell you that I still consider myself something of a left winger. (*This is to* CRISP.) Sorry about that business in the lift, by the way, Tommy. Well, one thing I remember clearly from my years and *years* of soccer is that if two players go for a ball which then goes into touch, there's never any doubt *among those players* which of them touched the ball last. I can't remember one occasion in all those years and *years* when the player who touched the ball last didn't realize it. So, what I want to know *is*—why is it that on Match of the Day, every time the bloody ball goes into touch, *both* players claim the throw-in for their own side? I merely ask for information. Is it because they are very, very stupid or is it because a dishonest advantage is as welcome as an honest one?

CHAMBERLAIN: Well, look, it's been a long evening, old chap—

ANDERSON: Tomorrow is another day, McKendrick.

MCKENDRICK: Tomorrow, in my experience, is usually the same day. Have a drink—

ANDERSON: No thank you.

MCKENDRICK: Here's a question for anthropologists. Name me a tribe which organizes itself into teams for sporting encounters and greets every score against their opponents with paroxysms of childish glee, whooping, dancing and embracing in an ecstasy of crowing self-congratulation in the very midst of their disconsolate fellows?—Who are these primitives who pile all their responses into the immediate sensation, unaware or uncaring of the long undulations of life's fortunes? Yes, you've got it! (*He chants the Match of the Day signature tune.*) It's the yob-of-the-month competition, entries on a postcard please. But the question

is—is it because they're working class, or is it because
financial greed has corrupted them? Or is it both?

ANDERSON: McKendrick, you are being offensive.

MCKENDRICK: Anderson is one of life's cricketers. Clap, clap.
(*He claps in a well-bred sort of way and puts on a well-bred
voice.*) Well played, sir. Bad luck, old chap. The comparison
with cricket may suggest to you that yob ethics are working
class.
(BROADBENT *comes up to* MCKENDRICK *and pushes him against
the wall.* MCKENDRICK *is completely unconcerned, escapes and
continues without pause.*)
But you would be quite wrong. Let me refer you to a
typical rugby team of Welsh miners. A score is acknowledged
with pride but with restraint, the scorer himself composing
his features into an expressionless mask lest he might be
suspected of exulting in his opponents' misfortune—my
God, it does the heart good, doesn't it? I conclude that yob
ethics are caused by financial greed.

ANDERSON: Don't be such an ass.
(MCKENDRICK *takes this as an intellectual objection.*)

MCKENDRICK: You think it's the adulation, perhaps? (*To* CRISP.)
Is it the adulation, Tommy, which has corrupted you?

CRISP: What's he flaming on about?

CHAMBERLAIN: Well I think it's time for my shut-eye.

CRISP: No, I want to know what he's saying about me. He's
giving me the needle.

ANDERSON: (*To* MCKENDRICK) May I remind you that you profess
to be something of a pragmatist yourself in matters of
ethics—

MCKENDRICK: Ah yes—I see—you think that because I don't
believe in reliable signposts on the yellow brick road to
rainbowland, you think I'm a bit of a yob myself—the
swift kick in the kneecap on the way up the academic ladder
—the Roy Broadbent of Stoke— (*To* BROADBENT.) Stoke's
my team, you know.

BROADBENT: Will you tell this stupid bugger his philosophy is
getting up my nostrils.

GRAYSON: You're not making much sense, old boy.

MCKENDRICK: Ah! Grayson here has a fine logical mind. He has

171

put his finger on the flaw in my argument, namely that the reason footballers are yobs may be nothing to do with being working class, or with financial greed, or with adulation, or even with being footballers. It may be simply that football attracts a certain kind of person, namely yobs—

(*This is as far as he gets when* BROADBENT *smashes him in the face.* MCKENDRICK *drops.*)

CRISP: Good on you, Roy.

(ANDERSON *goes to* MCKENDRICK *who is flat on the floor.*)

ANDERSON: McKendrick . . .

CHAMBERLAIN: Well, I'm going to bed.

(CHAMBERLAIN *goes through the connecting door into his own room and closes the door.*)

BROADBENT: He can't say that sort of thing and get away with it.

GRAYSON: Where's his room?

ANDERSON: On the third floor.

GRAYSON: Bloody hell.

CRISP: He's waking up.

BROADBENT: He's all right.

ANDERSON: Come on McKendrick.

(*They all lift* MCKENDRICK *to his feet.* MCKENDRICK *makes no protest. He's just about able to walk.*)

I'll take him down in the lift. (*He sees the typewriter in its case and says to* GRAYSON.) I'll come back for the typewriter. (*He leads* MCKENDRICK *towards the door.*)

MCKENDRICK: (*Mutters*) All right. I went too far. Let's talk about something else.

(*But* MCKENDRICK *keeps walking or staggering.* ANDERSON *opens* GRAYSON'S *door.*)

BROADBENT: Here. That bloody Jirasek. Just like you said.

ANDERSON: Yes.

BROADBENT: They don't teach you nothing at that place then.

ANDERSON: No.

(ANDERSON *helps* MCKENDRICK *out and closes the door.*)


11. THE COLLOQUIUM

ANDERSON *comes to the lectern. There is a Czech* CHAIRMAN *behind him.*

CHETWYN *is in the audience but* MCKENDRICK *is not. We arrive as*

ANDERSON *approaches the microphone.* ANDERSON *lays a sheaf of typewritten paper on the lectern.*

ANDERSON: I propose in this paper to take up a problem which many have taken up before me, namely the conflict between the rights of individuals and the rights of the community. I will be making a distinction between rights and rules.

(*We note that the* CHAIRMAN, *listening politely and intently, is suddenly puzzled. He himself has some papers and from these he extracts one, which is in fact the official copy of* ANDERSON'*s official paper. He starts looking at it. It doesn't take him long to satisfy himself that* ANDERSON *is giving a different paper. These things happen while* ANDERSON *speaks. At the same time the three* INTERPRETERS *in their booths, while speaking into their microphones as* ANDERSON *speaks, are also in some difficulty because they have copies of* ANDERSON'*s official paper.*)

I will seek to show that rules, in so far as they are related to rights, are a secondary and consequential elaboration of primary rights, and I will be associating rules generally with communities and rights generally with individuals. I will seek to show that a conflict between the two is generally a pseudo-conflict arising out of one side or the other pressing a pseudo-right. Although claiming priority for rights over rules—where they are in conflict—I will be defining rights as fictions acting as incentives to the adoption of practical values; and I will further propose that although these rights are fictions there is an obligation to treat them as if they were truths; and further, that although this obligation can be shown to be based on values which are based on fictions, there is an obligation to treat *that* obligation as though it were based on truth; and so on *ad infinitum.*

(*At this point the* CHAIRMAN *interrupts him.*)

CHAIRMAN: Pardon me—Professor—this is not your paper—

ANDERSON: In what sense? I am indisputably giving it.

CHAIRMAN: But it is not the paper you were invited to give.

ANDERSON: I wasn't invited to give a particular paper.

CHAIRMAN: You offered one.

ANDERSON: That's true.

CHAIRMAN: But this is not it.

ANDERSON: No. I changed my mind.

CHAIRMAN: But it is irregular.

ANDERSON: I didn't realize it mattered.

CHAIRMAN: It is a discourtesy.

ANDERSON: (*Taken aback*) Bad manners? I am sorry.

CHAIRMAN: You cannot give this paper. We do not have copies.

ANDERSON: Do you mean that philosophical papers require some sort of clearance?

CHAIRMAN: The interpreters cannot work without copies.

ANDERSON: Don't worry. It is not a technical paper. I will speak a little slower if you like. (ANDERSON *turns back to the microphone*.) If we decline to define rights as fictions, albeit with the force of truths, there are only two senses in which humans could be said to have rights. Firstly, humans might be said to have certain rights if they had collectively and mutually agreed to give each other these rights. This would merely mean that humanity is a rather large club with club rules, but it is not what is generally meant by human rights. It is not what Locke meant, and it is not what the American Founding Fathers meant when, taking the hint from Locke, they held certain rights to be unalienable—among them, life, liberty and the pursuit of happiness. The early Americans claimed these as the endowment of God—which is the *second* sense in which humans might be said to have rights. This is a view more encouraged in some communities than in others. I do not wish to dwell on it here except to say that it *is* a view and not a deduction, and that I do not hold it myself.

What strikes us is the consensus about an individual's rights put forward both by those who invoke God's authority and by those who invoke no authority at all other than their own idea of what is fair and sensible. The first Article of the American Constitution, guaranteeing freedom of religious observance, of expression, of the press, and of assembly, is closely echoed by Articles 28 and 32 of the no less admirable Constitution of Czechoslovakia, our generous hosts on this occasion. Likewise, protection from invasion of privacy, from unreasonable search and from interference with letters and correspondence guaranteed to the American people by Article 4 is likewise guaranteed to the Czech people by

Article 31.

(*The* CHAIRMAN, *who has been more and more uncomfortable,*
*leaves the stage at this point. He goes into the 'wings'. At some*
*distance from* ANDERSON, *but still just in earshot of* ANDERSON,
*i.e. one can hear* ANDERSON'*s words clearly if faintly, is a*
*telephone. Perhaps in a stage manager's office. We go with the*
CHAIRMAN *but we can still hear* ANDERSON.)

Is such a consensus remarkable? Not at all. If there is a
God, we his creations would doubtless subscribe to his
values. And if there is not a God, he, our creation, would
undoubtedly be credited with values which we think to be
fair and sensible. But what is fairness? What is sense? What
are these values which we take to be self-evident? And why
are they values?

### 12. INT. MCKENDRICK'S ROOM

MCKENDRICK *is fully dressed and coming round from a severe hangover.*
*His room is untidier than* ANDERSON'*s. Clothes are strewn about. His*
*suitcase, half full, is open. His briefcase is also in evidence.* MCKEN-
DRICK *looks at his watch, but it has stopped. He goes to the telephone*
*and dials.*

### 13. INT. ANDERSON'S ROOM

*The phone starts to ring. The camera pulls back from the phone and*
*we see that there are two men in the room, plainclothes* POLICEMEN,
*searching the room. They look at the phone but only for a moment, and*
*while it rings they continue quietly. They search the room very*
*discreetly. We see one carefully slide open a drawer and we cut away.*

### 14. THE COLLOQUIUM

*We have returned to* ANDERSON'*s paper. There is no* CHAIRMAN *on*
*stage.*

ANDERSON: Ethics were once regarded as a sort of monument, a
  ghostly Eiffel Tower constructed of Platonic entities like
  honesty, loyalty, fairness, and so on, all bolted together and
  consistent with each other, harmoniously stressed so as to
  keep the edifice standing up: an ideal against which we
  measured our behaviour. The tower has long been demolished.
  In our own time linguistic philosophy proposes that the

notion of, say, justice has no existence outside the ways in which we choose to employ the word, and indeed *consists* only of the way in which we employ it. In other words, that ethics are not the inspiration of our behaviour but merely the creation of our utterances.

(*Over the latter part of this we have gone back to the* CHAIRMAN *who is on the telephone. The* CHAIRMAN *is doing little talking and some listening.*)

And yet common observation shows us that this view demands qualification. A small child who cries 'that's not fair' when punished for something done by his brother or sister is apparently appealing to an idea of justice which is, for want of a better word, natural. And we must see that natural justice, however illusory, does inspire many people's behaviour much of the time. As an ethical utterance it seems to be an attempt to define a sense of rightness which is not simply derived from some other utterance elsewhere.

(*We cut now to a backstage area, but* ANDERSON's *voice is continuous, heard through the sort of P.A. system which one finds backstage at theatres.*

*The* CHAIRMAN *hurries along the corridor, seeking, and now finding a uniformed* 'FIREMAN', *a backstage official. During this* ANDERSON *speaks.*)

Now a philosopher exploring the difficult terrain of right and wrong should not be over impressed by the argument 'a child would know the difference'. But when, let us say, we are being persuaded that it is ethical to put someone in prison for reading or writing the wrong books, it is well to be reminded that you can persuade a man to believe almost anything provided he is clever enough, but it is much more difficult to persuade someone less clever. There is a sense of right and wrong which precedes utterance. It is individually experienced and it concerns one person's dealings with another person. From this experience we have built a system of ethics which is the sum of individual acts of recognition of individual right.

(*During this we have returned to* ANDERSON *in person. And at this point the* CHAIRMAN *re-enters the stage and goes and sits in his chair.* ANDERSON *continues, ignoring him.*)

If this is so, the implications are serious for a collective or
State ethic which finds itself in conflict with individual
rights, and seeks, in the name of the people, to impose its
values on the very individuals who comprise the State. The
illogic of this manoeuvre is an embarrassment to totalitarian
systems. An attempt is sometimes made to answer it by
consigning the whole argument to 'bourgeois logic', which
is a concept no easier to grasp than bourgeois physics or
bourgeois astronomy. No, the fallacy must lie elsewhere—
(*At this point loud bells, electric bells, ring. The fire alarm.
The* CHAIRMAN *leaps up and shouts.*)

CHAIRMAN: (*In Czech*) Don't panic! There appears to be a fire.
Please leave the hall in an orderly manner. (*In English.*) Fire!
Please leave quietly!

(*The philosophers get to their feet and start heading for the exit.*
ANDERSON *calmly gathers his papers up and leaves the stage.*)

15. INT. AIRPORT

*People leaving the country have to go through a baggage check. There
are at least three separate but adjacent benches at which customs men
and women search the baggage of travellers. The situation here is as
follows:*

*At the first bench* CHETWYN *is in mid-search.*

*At the second bench* ANDERSON *is in mid-search.*

*At the third bench a traveller is in mid-search.*

*There is a short queue of people waiting for each bench. The leading
man in the queue waiting for the third bench is* MCKENDRICK. *The
search at this third bench is cursory.*

*However,* ANDERSON *is being searched very thoroughly. We begin on*
ANDERSON. *We have not yet noted* CHETWYN.

*At* ANDERSON's *bench a uniformed customs* WOMAN *is examining the
contents of his suitcase, helped by a uniformed customs* MAN. *At the
same time a plainclothes* POLICEMAN *is very carefully searching
everything in* ANDERSON's *briefcase.*

*We see the customs* MAN *take a cellophane wrapped box of chocolates
from* ANDERSON's *case. He strips off the cellophane and looks at the
chocolates and then he digs down to look at the second layer of
chocolates.* ANDERSON *watches this with amazement. The chocolate
box is closed and put back in the case. Meanwhile a nest of wooden*

*dolls, the kind in which one doll fits inside another, is reduced to its*
*components.*
*The camera moves to find* MCKENDRICK *arriving at the third desk.*
*There is no plainclothes man there. The customs* OFFICER *there opens*
*his briefcase and flips, in a rather cursory way, through* MCKENDRICK's
*papers. He asks* MCKENDRICK *to open his case. He digs about for a*
*moment in* MCKENDRICK's *case.*
*Back at* ANDERSON's *bench the plainclothes* MAN *is taking* ANDERSON's
*wallet from* ANDERSON's *hand. He goes through every piece of paper*
*in the wallet.*
*We go back to* MCKENDRICK's *bench to find* MCKENDRICK *closing his*
*case and being moved on.* MCKENDRICK *turns round to* ANDERSON *to*
*speak.*

MCKENDRICK: You picked the wrong queue, old man. Russian
    roulette. And Chetwyn.
    (*We now discover* CHETWYN *who is going through a similar*
    *search to* ANDERSON's. *He has a plainclothes* MAN *too. This* MAN
    *is looking down the spine of a book from* CHETWYN's *suitcase.*
    *We now return to* ANDERSON's *bench. We find that the customs*
    MAN *has discovered a suspicious bulge in the zipped compartment*
    *on the underside of the lid of* ANDERSON's *suitcase.* ANDERSON's
    *face tells us that he has a spasm of anxiety. The bulge suggests*
    *something about the size of* HOLLAR's *envelope. The customs*
    MAN *zips open the compartment and extracts the copy of*
    MCKENDRICK's *girly magazine.* ANDERSON *is embarrassed.*
    *We return to* CHETWYN *whose briefcase is being searched paper*
    *by paper. The customs* OFFICIAL *searching his suitcase finds a*
    *laundered shirt, nicely ironed and folded. He opens the shirt*
    *up and discovers about half a dozen sheets of writing-paper.*
    *Thin paper with typewriting on it. Also a photograph of a man.*
    *The plainclothes* MAN *joins the customs* OFFICIAL *and he starts*
    *looking at these pieces of paper. He looks up at* CHETWYN
    *whose face has gone white.*)


16. INT. AEROPLANE
*The plane is taxiing.*
MCKENDRICK *and* ANDERSON *are sitting together.*
MCKENDRICK *looks shocked.*
MCKENDRICK: Silly bugger. Honestly.

ANDERSON: It's all right—they'll put him on the next plane.

MCKENDRICK: To Siberia.

ANDERSON: No, no, don't be ridiculous. It wouldn't look well for them, would it? All the publicity. I don't think there's anything in Czech law about being in possession of letters to Amnesty International and the U.N. and that sort of thing. They couldn't treat Chetwyn as though he were a Czech national anyway.

MCKENDRICK: Very unpleasant for him though.

ANDERSON: Yes.

MCKENDRICK: He took a big risk.

ANDERSON: Yes.

MCKENDRICK: I wouldn't do it. Would you?

ANDERSON: No. He should have known he'd be searched.

MCKENDRICK: Why did they search you?

ANDERSON: They thought I might have something.

MCKENDRICK: Did you have anything?

ANDERSON: I did in a way.

MCKENDRICK: What was it?

ANDERSON: A thesis. Apparently rather slanderous from the State's point of view.

MCKENDRICK: Where did you hide it?

ANDERSON: In your briefcase.

(*Pause.*)

MCKENDRICK: You what?

ANDERSON: Last night. I'm afraid I reversed a principle.

(MCKENDRICK *opens his briefcase and finds* HOLLAR'*s envelope.* ANDERSON *takes it from him.* MCKENDRICK *is furious.*)

MCKENDRICK: You utter bastard.

ANDERSON: I thought you would approve.

MCKENDRICK: Don't get clever with me. (*He relapses, shaking.*) Jesus. It's not quite playing the game is it?

ANDERSON: No, I suppose not. But they were very unlikely to search *you.*

MCKENDRICK: That's not the bloody point.

ANDERSON: I thought it was. But you could be right. Ethics is a very complicated business. That's why they have these congresses.

(*The plane picks up speed on the runway towards take-off.*)